WILD
GEESE

Also by Nan Shepherd

The Quarry Wood (1928)
The Weatherhouse (1930)
A Pass in the Grampians (1933)
In the Cairngorms (1934)
The Living Mountain (1977)

WILD GEESE

A Collection of
Nan Shepherd's Writing

Edited by
Charlotte Peacock

Galileo Publishers
16 Woodlands Road
Great Shelford
Cambridge CB22 5LW
UK

www.galileopublishing.co.uk

ISBN 978-1-903385-79-1

First published in the UK 2018

1 2 3 4 5 6 7 8 9

Printed in the EU

Contents

Introduction

by Charlotte Peacock

'I don't like writing, really. In fact, I very rarely write. No. I never do short stories and articles', Nan Shepherd confessed in 1933. 'I only write when I feel that there's something that simply must be written'.[1] Certainly, Shepherd was not one to shout for the sake of making noise: her oeuvre is slender. During her lifetime (1893-1981) she published just five major works.

First, between 1928 and 1933, came three complex and remarkable novels: *The Quarry Wood*; *The Weatherhouse*; and *A Pass in the Grampians*. Declared Scotland's answer to Virginia Woolf,[2] Shepherd then showed what she could do with verse, producing *In the Cairngorms* in 1934. Those hoping for a renaissance in Scottish letters were encouraged. A few more writers of Shepherd's 'power and originality' and Scotland might yet have a literature of its own.[3]

Readers and critics eagerly waiting for what Miss Shepherd did next, however, were disappointed. She appeared to have lost her voice. By the late 1960s her books were out of print and she had slipped into literary obscurity.

'Why, I wonder, did you give up literature so early?', the poet, Rachel Annand Taylor asked in 1959.[4] 'It just didn't come to me anymore', Shepherd answered, when pressed, years later. [5]

But Shepherd had not given up. Like the skein she describes in 'Wild Geese in Glen Callater', which, 'buffeted and mishandled' by the wind, turned back before disappearing into 'diaphanous cloud', her flight was merely deflected.[6]

Towards the end of the Second World War something else simply *had* to be written. An enlightened series of meditations on her beloved Cairngorms, Shepherd's last book was ahead of its time. Courteously rejected in 1945, the manuscript lay in waiting for over thirty years, until she decided the world was ready for it. First published in 1977, *The Living Mountain* is now considered a masterpiece of landscape literature.

'You can never know if your work is positively good until you've been dead a century or so', the historian and writer Agnes Mure Mackenzie told Shepherd after the publication of *The Quarry Wood*.[7] It has taken less than half that time for Shepherd's literary legacy to be given the recognition it deserves. The first woman writer to grace a Scottish banknote, all five of her major works are once again in print. A volume of her other writings is timely — if not overdue.

During those forty-three years between books, speech did return to Shepherd, albeit intermittently. And despite what she said in 1933, it took the form of a short story and a host of articles. She also produced more verse. Gathered here is a selection of these writings, as well as some earlier pieces. For someone who professed not to like writing, each text, in whichever medium she chooses, reveals her artistry.

Her habit of engaging readers with casually conversational asides — 'Why I should begin by writing of his drollery

I hardly know' – is deceptive.[8] Every narrative is carefully structured. She is a master of opening lines: 'Marion Angus was not wholly human';[9] 'Charles Murray was a man one could not miss in company'.[10] She can conjure a character, sometimes in no more than a series of deftly drawn strokes. Miss Abercrombie Gaunt is a 'clothes-pole figure', 'hard as a harrow'; Betsy 'hoarse and black', 'dargs like a man'.[11] She uses imagery rooted in the Scottish landscape to sharpen portraits of its people. James Downie's 'tales had a delicious tang — like bog-myrtle or juniper'.[12]

Her descriptions of the natural world are as vividly wrought. Scotland's blue can be 'azure thinned out…beaten to a transparency of itself' or seems to be substance, lying 'like the bloom on a plum, or the pile of plush'.[13] Wild geese fade out into cloud, growing 'fainter and fainter, now a silverpoint, at last a wraith, a memory of shape'.[14]

Light haunts Shepherd's work. In *Descent from the Cross,* its presence is made tangible:

> It was a day so filled with light that the stubble shone and in the sun-saturated
> atmosphere floated gossamers, thistledown and the seeds of willowherb, airier
> than snowflakes, more delicate than moths, as though light had flaked itself off in filament and frond and brushed their cheeks…[15]

Written in 1942, at ten thousand words *Descent from the Cross* is a long, short story. Readers familiar with Shepherd's novels will recognise her trademarks: her use of language — English prose and dialect for dialogue; her wit; her compassion for her cast; and a female protagonist challenging convention in a small Scottish community. Like the multi-perspective, layered narratives of the novels, too, *Descent from the Cross* demands close reading. Then all its surfaces are seen as surfaces, its significance revealed.

Its significance was not lost on her friend, the novelist Neil Gunn, for whom her story developed a kind of legendary power. He was certain she could 'write a greater story now than ever before'.[16] But Shepherd was done with fiction. Most novels left her cold. What excited her was writing that managed to achieve what she strove for herself – to transfigure raw material into something universal — to 'irradiate the common' as she put it.[17] Famously reticent, it never occurred to her she had a gift for doing exactly that.

Instead she toiled to promote other Scottish writers whose work she deemed valuable, not purely as part of any literary renaissance, but universally, and for the future. Sharp-eyed Shepherd often saw what others missed or misunderstood. At a time when his linguistic experiments with vernacular verse were much maligned, she proved a prescient critic of Hugh MacDiarmid's poetry. Her lengthy defence of his work is printed here in its entirety, alongside tributes to Marion Angus and Charles Murray.

Poetry did not come easily to Shepherd herself. 'It seems to me', she wrote to Gunn, 'to hold in intensest being the very heart of all experience; and though I have now and then glimpsed something of that burning heart of life...always when I try to put these things into words they elude me. The result is slight and small'.[18] Most of the poems contained in *In the Cairngorms* were written, in a state she likened to 'possession',[19] between 1930 and 1934. She was rarely 'possessed' again.

At the heart of this book is some of Shepherd's unpublished poetry. Earlier lyrics, 'The Trees', 'The Dryad', 'Street Urchins' and 'Arthur's Seat', like those included in her anthology, were ticked in her poetry notebook, suggesting she originally intended them for publication. Ultimately, only those inspired by the Massif or written while she was in the hills themselves, made it into the collection.

Neither 'The Burning Glass' nor 'Union'[20] appear in the sonnet series closing *In the Cairngorms*. 'Very few people understand them', Shepherd said of her sonnets, 'which makes me feel better'.[21] She never married. Nor did she ever reveal the name of the man for whom they were written. This was an 'illicit love'.[22] Less oblique than others, 'The Burning Glass' expresses the fear and effect of discovery: 'O, I could watch my world blaze up and perish'.[23]

'Union' is explicit on the subject of consummation. Sensually suggestive, it is threaded with the intricate metaphysical quality of many of Shepherd's lyrics. The poem is not in Shepherd's notebook, but was certainly written by 1931 as it was among others she enclosed in a letter to Neil Gunn that year. '…Know'st/Though more, still less'… In those lines there is already something of a refrain of *The Living Mountain*: 'Knowing another is endless…The thing to be known grows with the knowing'.[24]

Four of Shepherd's finest poems, 'Achiltibuie', 'Next Morning', 'On a Still Morning' and 'Rhu Coigach', were composed in 1950. Tucked, loose, into her manuscript notebook, they were inspired by a visit to the north-west coast of Scotland. They are anything but 'slight and small'. Like 'Falketind' (written in 1937 on a trip to Norway) they reveal a mind still passionately engaged with nature and the elements. Three were penned on successive mornings, each offering different, elementally illuminated perspectives. All share a common theme: to look out is to go in.

'Movements of being',[25] as Shepherd describes this traffic between the physical, outer landscape and spiritual inwardness distilled in *The Living Mountain,* she now crystallises in verse. In 'Achiltibuie', surfaces merge, blurring until the rocks:

Are a fire of blue, a pulse of power, a beat
In energy, the sea dissolves,
And I too melt, am timeless, a pulse of light.[26]

Echoing the rhythm of the waves, like many of Shepherd's lines, they linger long in the ear.

Water, woods, rocks, plants, pools and peaks permeate her poems and prose. Those things that really mattered to Shepherd reverberate in her writing. Her landscape — Scotland's North-East, where she lived all her life; her perception of the primordial 'like some ancient earth magic'[27] in her living encounters with bird or animal life; brushes with the 'elementals', hurling us back, setting 'the puny world in its true perspective'.[28] People mattered too, whether known to her or not. Her ability to draw them out and capture their quirks is conspicuous in the snapshots of 'Things I Shall Never Know'. Shepherd newsed with everyone, regardless of class.

Shepherd thought more of her lectureship at Aberdeen's teacher-training centre than she did of her work as a writer.[29] 'Schools and Schoolmistresses' shows her interest in her students long outlived their time at the institution. Quietly anarchic, Shepherd saw her role more as a vocation — to discourage her students from conforming to societal expectation and 'get leave to live'.[30]

Shepherd found her way into freedom in the hills. She loved tramping in open country as she loved few things on earth. In fact, much of her material was worked out and wrought into shape while she was 'on the tramp', she said.[31] Because, of course, there was art, too. Although it was 'the grasp of the essential meaning and nature and being of whatever one turns into art', that really mattered.[32]

Her earliest pieces reflect a muscular mind that would turn

from institutional religion, to the eastern philosophies woven through *The Living Mountain*. This was knowledge, she realised, that could not be gleaned from books alone but from living, 'all the way through'.[33] And so she did.

PART I

Descent from the Cross

1

Born in 1902, Elizabeth was too young for the first World War. By the time she reached college the War Veterans were returning, demigods, demidevils, a people apart. Elizabeth began to be aware she was shut out from something, but there was no sesame for that door. She stayed out and went on working. She worked like a puppy at a sandbank. By 1928 (when this story begins) she was organising the welfare services of a big paper mill. She ran to conferences and read reports and reviews, but tested all the bright new ideas with a level sobriety of judgment. The millgirls loved her like a sister.

"Our Bet's got her horns out," said her mother. "She was always a grand hand at arranging people's lives. It's a great mercy there's jobs about that lets her do it in peace."

Not only in peace, but to the tune of a salary that made her uncles and forty-second cousins, the small farmers and country carriers from whom she was sprung, chuckle with approval. They were proud of their Betsy, and what was more, they liked her, too; which isn't always the case with the ones that get on. A jolly brown girl, freckles on her nose and big teeth, no beauty, but with a frank open face that won immediate trust, and steady eyes. Red-headed, to be sure, but red heads kept you out of languor. Shoulders squared, she marched on life with such zest that she had nearly forgotten the door without the sesame. Yet sometimes she had dreams; she dreamed of engulfing seas, but no seas engulfed her. Busy, practical and gay, prodigal of herself in good works, like a little hill pony for sturdy strength, she lived on the solid earth and loved her life.

So, when she told her people she was going to marry that lank, stuck-up lad — half a corpse he looked even then — not one among her folk but thought her ill-advised. Not that they said the likes of that to Betsy, who was earning a mint, and had the right to keep her man in idleness if so she pleased. Her mother sniffed with one side of her nose in a way she had, and asked: "And which of the pair of you will stay at home and mind the bairns, I should like to be informed."

Elizabeth, who had a temper, kept it. She knew that the question was not a question, but a plummet dropped in the gulf between Elizabeth as her parents had made her, and Elizabeth as she had made herself; for already this marriage had swung her whole universe away from her habitual self. In a sallow hag-ridden prisoner of war, whose body had been released but not his mind — indeed whose body was still in bondage to the shucks he had eaten and the exposure he had endured — Elizabeth had found a freedom so immense that she trembled before it; and she resented angrily the conclaves of old men and spinsters who talked her man over. No wound, no pension, neither crippled nor blinded nor bedridden – what sort of man was he then, to let himself be kept by his wife? A disordered stomach seemed a queer sort of reason for living off a woman's wages.

"No guts, that's what ails the lad," they said.

"What business is it of theirs?" cried Elizabeth in fury.

"They'll make it their business, whether or no," said her

mother, realist to the bone, "so you'd best tell them all about it to begin with."

She hated the need to justify her lover to her tribe. Old men! she thought, baring her teeth. But she was of the tribe; their forthright speech was her own. She knew that the old men were proud of her — their bonny Liz, kind and capable, a spirity lass that warmed you like a nip of Scotch. Half the things they said about her marriage were for the pleasure of her retorts.

"He's just like any other body," said Uncle Benjie. "A gey, ordinary kind o' chiel."

As though, scoffed Elizabeth, he knew all the great ones of the earth.

"A gey few," said Benjie. "I've spoken wi' the Marquis."

"Well," said Elizabeth, "he looks ordinary enough to me."

"O ay," said Benjie, "but he gets his name in the paper."

"Well, so will my man," said Elizabeth. "Just you wait and you'll see."

"And not even a stick leg," continued Uncle Benjie. "I thought I was to see a lad wi' a stick leg. What's come o' the timmer leg, lassie?"

"Ach," said Elizabeth, "it's his intimmers, Benjie." And she flung a phrase over her shoulder that caused the old fellow to double up with mirth. A dozen times in the evening he muttered over to himself "stickit intimmers," and, catching Elizabeth's eye, winked. But Elizabeth's face was stony.

At the wedding feast, Tommy made a sorry bridegroom.

"Ye were some ill," as Uncle Benjie said, "for forgetting he was there." He had not the knack of speech, not with these country folk, forcey with their drinking as with their tongues, and thanks to his connached stomach he couldn't even win their respect by the way he tackled his dram.

"Neither dram nor conversation — you might as well be

with the nowt in the field," they thought. When he rose to the toast, he didn't even habber, a graceful thing in a bridegroom, reassuring to the herd. Four drawling chilly sentences, and he was down again. "What was you lang-nebbit word?" whispered a cousin — and Elizabeth was on her feet, laughing, flinging back the challenge of their indifferent eyes.

"I don't see why a bride can't speak for herself," she cried. And then Tommy heard her prophesy before them all the fame that waited for his book — the book that was his secret and his doom, that had been shaping itself in his tormented mind ever since he hung by the wrists in a German forest.

They cheered her with a bellow; but it wasn't the grand future they were cheering, it was the present, it was Elizabeth herself with her flushed face and shining eyes. When, seven years later, they buried her man (and Tommy Martin remained "yon man of Bet's" to most of his wife's relations, who hardly saw him from the day they married him to the day they saw Elizabeth stand erect and quiet beside his open grave), one and another recalled her sparkling face as she prophesied his fame. "Ay, and she believed it, too, that was the mischief o't."

2

But it was not the mischief of it. That she believed in Tommy, and he in her belief in him, began his slow release from captivity, which as yet had been nominal. She was the first on whom he had been able to discharge that wood — a handful of defiant boys in the power of a confident enemy. Idiots! They had committed the folly of telling the truth, in wartime, about themselves, and there they were, self-convicted engineers, told off to make enemy munitions. And to counter their refusal, the wood. Six of them hung up by the wrists, toes just off the ground. Life ended there — some other man was born. And between his two faints — Tommy brooded, his slow voice running on in the dusk — some sort of apocalypse. He couldn't explain it, nor why it was him it should have come to. Delirium, perhaps. But no, his brain was never clearer. He seemed to be out of the body, pain was gone: and with superhuman clarity he saw the truth of things. Then, he supposed, he must have fainted again. He remembered the untying and his vain attempt to stand — he pitched over under an officer's horse.

There were two years of prison camps after that, but since that moment of illumination nothing had really mattered but getting it into words. He knew, now, the meaning of human destiny.

The first time she heard the story, Elizabeth thrust out her hand in the dark and touched him. It was a tough hand. He held it and grew calmer.

"But, you know," he said apologetically, in his low voice, "I did see something then — understand something. Something pretty fundamental. If I could work it out, I see it as the basis of a whole philosophy of living. It was a sort of crucifixion. And I think — the thing I saw — could save mankind. If I could work it out."

He had gone into newspaper work on his return; it seemed to offer the experience he needed. But the provincialism, the deadening, exhausting round of trivialities! And then he was never well. He had eaten dirt and it stood between him and the good food that should have nourished his body.

Elizabeth, in her rare moments went fey, leaping into the future without a glance. She leaped then.

("Havers," said Elizabeth's mother to her father — Mrs Archibald knew more about her daughter than Elizabeth dreamed. "It was our Bet that did the asking, you take my word for that. And yon quiet laddie didn't take it easy, either. But, bless me, she's that sort.")

So the first year of their marriage was perfect for Elizabeth. They had an old cottage out of town, and Tommy worked steadily at his book, but welcomed her home from work with odd surprises — rare food or flowers or the table set in the garden — imaginative things unknown to Elizabeth's hardier breed. She ate new kinds of food — "gentry's food," Uncle Benjie would have called it — and with a shy disarming smile Tommy would blame it on his wretched digestion.

Only one thing marred her happiness — that the book grew so slowly. Sheets covered with notes — yes; but nothing coherent. Nothing she could read and weigh.

"Not even Chapter One yet?" she would ask, leaning her chin upon his hair.

One day he said, "Perhaps you'd like to look at this."

"Chapter One?" she cried, her eyes gleaming as she took the sheaf of papers.

With his shy smile he said, "Chapter Five, I think."

"Oh, don't you write a book from the beginning?"

He said slowly, "I'm working it into shape."

She read with mounting excitement. It was tart, firm writing. Each word told. "No wonder he took months," she thought, "to this." It was good — without favour, it was good. And a sense of tremendous issues flooded her mind.

"Look," she said, "this stands alone. It's a finished thing, by itself. You want to be known before the big book comes — let's send this to one of the *Reviews*."

When it was accepted, she said, "Of course! I knew that it was good." And in a dream of joy she walked with Tommy over the September fields. It was a day so filled with light that the stubble shone and in the sun-saturated atmosphere floated gossamers, thistledown and the seeds of willowherb, airier than snowflakes, more delicate than moths, as though light had flaked itself off in filament and frond and brushed their cheeks like a tangible presence. Everything, she felt, was coming to fulfilment, the book would go on and on and conquer the world. She didn't know even yet what Tommy's philosophy was. It was vague to her — beautiful and solemn. When he talked of it, new horizons opened before her, but this was less from intellectual apprehension than from the emotion induced by his low vibrating voice and her sense of sharing in a profound experience. At last she was inside. She could hardly bear her happiness as she walked through the sun-soaked fields, and saw the book growing and growing till it re-vitalised the world.

9

3

The book, however, did not grow. Tommy toiled at it, wresting from his uneasy brain a word here, a word there, building them painfully into sentences that the following week he smashed. He covered many pages with oddments, but they remained incongruous. Chapter Five alone had form.

His health, too, which had improved enormously, grew worse again in the hard east Spring. He tried to hide from Elizabeth the pain and nausea that wrung him, keeping himself in hand till she was gone to work, and then collapsing in exhaustion. Often it seemed to him that his whole day's business consisted in gathering himself together against her return, and Elizabeth, whose health was perfect, did not guess.

Besides, the comfort she brought him had softened his apocalyptic fervour. Still in his teens when he was captured, a boy of singular innocence of mind whom life had hardly touched, he had been exposed unarmed to its indignities and degradations, and, till he met Elizabeth, had gone sustained by an exaltation. Now she had released him from horror, and, by such gentle degrees that he had not yet perceived it, from the need of exaltation also. Sometimes, by fasting (but that was easy), and by discipline of his wandering attention, he strove to induce the moment of vision. The mood came, the sense of seeing deep into truth, but what that truth was he could ever quite discern.

In April he fell ill with gastritis, and his mother-in-law came to nurse him. Mrs Archibald was a foursquare Scot, with bones like rocks and a face large out of all proportion to her height. She regarded her son-in-law with a kindly contempt, which he returned, putting manners in place of the kindness. Elizabeth's family riled him. They were as rude as a blatter of sleet, and he grudged their animal soundness and animal insensitivity. Refusing his cornflour, he muttered that Elizabeth would bring him a patent food he craved.

"Well, and that's what she won't do," said Mrs Archibald sharply. "That things costs money."

"And what's money between Elizabeth and me?" he asked. Wasn't he using her money in trust — in a sacred trust — to make himself strong for the great work he was to write? But spoken aloud, the sentiment sounded odd. An audience altered its relevance. He listened to its doubtful echo on the air and supposed Mrs Archibald would take it with dudgeon.

"Bet," said Mrs Archibald reasonably, "would buy you the king's crown if she had the cash and wanted you to have it. Don't I know she's a terror? But that's no cause for us to take advantage."

The subtlety of the *us* (unintentional on Mrs Archibald's part) surprised him into pleasure. To be ranged with her mother against an abandoned Elizabeth moved in him a gentle sense of fun. Besides, a philosopher, fretted by the plain speech of a woman! A smile played on his thin face and he said, with more warmth in his tone than he had yet used to her:

"Ach, mother-in-law, away home with you."

"I'll go home quick enough, my lad, once you're able to be

up and writing at that book that's to make all our fortunes."

This version of his labours was novel, and caused Tommy to say, "Oh it's a fortune I'm to make, is it?"

" 'Deed'," said Mrs Archibald plainly, "and I've never expected it myself. It takes a deal of wit to make a fortune, be it by a book or any other road. But Bet has set her heart on it, you'd best be trauchlin' on, you might make a hit, who knows. The folks that read the books have funny tastes, I often say."

The next morning, towards eleven, Tommy dragged himself into his clothes and crept downstairs and out. A faint mist of green was in the hollows of the sown fields, a faint powdering of green on the birches. Fresh and chill and pure, April stood there, lovely beyond all his remembering. He gasped, and doubled over with weakness in the quickening air. Back in bed, he lay aching from exhaustion, but fought the need to sleep till he heard Mrs Archibald's solid step upon the landing. When she came in he was seated against pillows, his manuscript in front of him and his pencil making senseless trails across the paper.

"I'm at your fortune," he said, without raising his eyes.

"If you'd lie down and rest you'd be better able for your cornflour," she said severely.

Whether by pique or desire of the April he had glimpsed, in a few days he was able to walk again, and Mrs Archibald went home.

Now that he had recovered, Tommy worked very hard at the book. But in the weakness of convalescence, his devils came back at him, and again Elizabeth delivered him. After such spectral nights (she going sound and fresh to a day of exacting work) he could do little in the morning but lie in the sun or wander among trees, savouring with his body the exquisite sense of release she gave him. One morning he had wandered thus among young birches, that were hung with a thousand crystal drops of rain. The sun glowed and blazed in them, and the air was filled with the tart good smell of wet birch. A blackbird sang exultantly, bees zoomed above the clover, life was bursting on every side; and his heart leaped in tumult, he wanted to be part of this force of creation. Write! Write! But what am I to write, he pondered. What have I to write? As though the blaze of sun in the myriad crystals illumined his own inner self, he began to review the contents of his mind; and with the force of a revelation it came to him that he had no philosophy to offer the world, no book to write, nothing to say. And again he felt a sense of release. No more agonising struggle for words; words that refused him because there was no task for them to perform. No horrible responsibility towards the fellow-men he was to redeem by his proclamation of truth. What! he had been living on a false pretension! There would be no book, Chapter Five was all. I must tell Elizabeth, he thought. But he could not. He didn't want to tell her. He wanted nothing but to savour each moment as it passed, being, merely being, set free from all preoccupation. He surrendered himself to the world as he had surrendered himself to her, and in the surrender was the same release. To be nothing, not to matter, to have no importance — how sane it was, and good. He had never really lived till that morning.

The elation passed; and a deep dismay succeeded. He, a nobody, who had agonised upon his tree? But he saw plainly now that it was so. His was no crucifixion, merely an accident. You must be slung up because you are you, not because you happen to be on the spot, if you are to save men. And with the pitiless clarity of a sane man, he saw that this thing had merely happened to him; it had no inner necessity. He stared for a long time at this stripped version of himself.

The mood of humiliation passed also. A trick of his indolent mind, to escape the labour demanded by the book! And soberly, with a stiff lip, he sat down again, to castigate himself into the writing of it. But in a few days he knew beyond all cavil that the book was a dream. He had nothing to say.

So now he must tell Elizabeth.

4

Telling Elizabeth was harder than he foresaw, because she refused to be told. He was ill, he was worn-out, lying fallow was good for him. "Will you stop," he wanted to shout, "believing in me?" Yet as his mind went round in endless circles, he knew that her bright belief in him had been the condition of his release — that because of it he stood here now, a sane man, done with his prison. He was off the cross, an ordinary fellow, with damaged guts, no job and not much training, who had lived for nearly two years off a woman. His face of a dreaming boy, that had beguiled Elizabeth, changed rapidly. Its lines hardened, misery ate into it and irony whipped it.

Trying to convince her, he twisted phrases in his mouth, and at each mouthful the taste grew bitterer and his abasement more profound. He had lived off her charity, hadn't he? "What's money between me and Elizabeth?" Well, now he knew; and the knowledge sent him back in a fever to his pen, to write anything at all that would salvage his manhood. In vain. He could write nothing, or nothing saleable, which was what mattered now. He winced at the thought of his mother-in-law, remembering how light-heartedly he had derided a philosophy whose foundations were in money. How he had despised these relations of Elizabeth because their talk was all of prices and wages! What is a man worth? they asked, and the answer was simple and plain and utterly damnable. Yet here he was clutching for salvation at a little cash, which remained quite beyond his reach. He earned nothing. He was no happy journalist, writing with ease and candour; and when he wrestled for things to say, he could not eat, his nerves were raw, finally he subsided in a sick exhaustion that sent him back to bed, filled Elizabeth with solicitude and himself with shame.

Lying there, he fell a-wondering what happened to a man subsidised by his government to write a book, of his own choice, which he found it was not in him to write. Elizabeth, he saw, would hold him to it or exact a substitute he could not provide.

"Ach, Tammy lad," she would say, falling into the country speech she loved, "let the book bide a while. You can't round up your thoughts like a puckle stirks. Yon German chiel took till the day he died to write his *Faust*. Sharp your teeth on that my man, and tell me now, what am I going to do with yon young Jane I told you about last night. She bids fair to get over me."

For there was no resisting Elizabeth. Her head full of projects, her heart warm and vivid with plots for other people's good, smiling her comfortable smile, never abashed, since there was always a new expedient when she blundered, never discouraged, since folk were so various and exciting, she took it for granted that he would listen to all her tales, discuss her experiments and give advice about her "cases." It was good for his self-respect — until one day he began to wonder if that was not exactly why she did it, if he too, was not a "case," being gently managed for his own good.

And at just that juncture she edged him back upon the book.

"I tell you," he said bitterly, "I can't write the book. You can will courage into a poltroon, but you can't will creative genius into a man who hasn't it. You refuse to see that you've married a small man instead of a big one. Sorry, but there it is. No good blinking facts, is there?"

"Tammy," she said, "you're a great gomeril. I *know* you can do it."

Elizabeth, he was coming to see, simply couldn't believe in failure. God, what a creed! Life needs the dark slow decay of countless myriad frustrations to provide a soil for growth. But she wanted everyone to have the happiness of success. Before her tireless optimism he grew stark afraid. Her touch on him was as gentle as a nosing calfie's; but persistent. A free man, he had supposed? Well, there was a plain way of release; he must get some work.

"Bet, be sensible about this. I'm off my cross, for good and all. You should be thankful. I've found myself out before I settled into a poseur for life. And it's time I did a little ordinary living now. Earned a living, in fact."

He set to work looking for a job. Autumn had come, with blustering gales that went through his thin body as though it were paper. Going out from the shelter Elizabeth had provided for him, he saw other thin men, pursuing the same quest as himself, hungry, disillusioned and hopeless men, with wives and children dependent on them. Nineteen-thirty was drawing to its unhappy close. Shabby men hung about street corners, shabby men went from door to door offering writing-pads for sale, long queues waiting with a damnable patience outside works and Labour Exchanges, and Tommy felt, as he pulled his coat collar up and talked with them, that even if a job were available for him he would be constrained to give it over to one of these others, who had no Elizabeth to shelter them.

Elizabeth herself said, "Laddie, can't you let it be? We can't take the meat out of another man's mou'." And when they sat over their fire by night and told each other the things they had seen during the day, Elizabeth, her heart quick to succour all the misery she had been in touch with, would say, "Tam, lad, there's craiturs that would have neither bite nor sup without the dole, and we have plenty."

"Your money," he said.

"Well, and if? What's the odds? It's yours too. I'm yours, amn't I, and all I have? As though I wouldn't give you anything!"

"Yes," he said, "you must be God Almighty, mustn't you? In you I live, move and have my being. You would like to give me my very breath. But what about me? It's not so simple to be always the one who takes."

Deep within him, all the same, he knew that their bargain was not so one-sided as that; and when she didn't gainsay the point, he conceded it to some bitter thought. He had given her vicarious experience (a thrill, he put it to himself). She was like a child playing in a wood, with secret meanings for the things that everyone could see, and he, as her secret, was beginning to wonder if she was capable of experience for herself at all. His own, he realised, was only just begun.

He felt older now than Elizabeth, immeasurably more mature.

At last one day he had the chance of a minor post on a minor provincial paper a hundred miles away. Elizabeth was aghast.

"But Tommy, you can't go away. I can't do without you. You can't do this."

"I must have some work, you know, Bet." There was a small smile on his lips that she could not quite read. She said.

"Why don't you write your war experiences? Look at all these war books — pouring out. They're selling by the thousand. You've told me things — they would make a book."

"There was Chapter Five," he said.

18

"But expand it. Give them details, not philosophy. Personal things. The sort of thing you've told me."

"I can't exploit that ... So you don't want me to go away, Bet?"

"*Want* you to go!"

"Not even for good?"

"For good?"

"Well, you married a potential winner and I don't see why you should be called on to back a loser."

"Are you in your sane senses, Tommy?"

"I suppose it would let you down rather badly in front of your family," he went on remorselessly. "Own up to them that you'd backed a wrong 'un. It would hurt your pride, I know. Still, there's more at stake than pride. Bet, you married a ghost — someone who never existed. So now you're tied to me. If we're to go on living together it's me you have to live with, not the world-famous author. And I'm a pretty poor specimen. So for any sake don't stick to me because you don't want your folks to know that they saw through me sooner than you did."

Elizabeth, however, wasn't having any heroics. She laughed heartily and said, "My folks would be considerably more set by the ears if we separated than they'll ever be over your failure to write a book. In my family, my lad, husbands and wives live together and there's an end to that."

A free man, thought Tommy grimly. She needed him too much to let him go. She believed still that she could inspire him, she wanted him to be inspired — to take fire from her as he took food. Always, he thought again, the one that takes. His small, guarded smile crept over his face, and he said, "So you would like me to write a war book?"

"Have a shot at it anyway," said Elizabeth, smiling down on him. She felt very happy. There had been an obscure conflict between them and she had triumphed. She began to plan the book.

Soon she asked him to make some notes for her in the Public Library. She was reading a paper and had so little time to collect her material. Some statistics she needed.

"Devilling for you?" he asked, with his guarded smile. "Of course I'll devil."

Then there was an article to find for her in a weekly, all the growing literature of sociology to explore for things she ought to be in touch with. Her work was expanding rapidly. It was good sound work and took all the time and thought she could give it, and more. So the odd jobs she asked of him were not merely salve to his self-respect.

He needed the salve. The war book went no better than the philosophy. He had no popular touch, on paper his experiences went stale. Even Elizabeth recognised that no publisher would look at it. She induced him to isolate some of the episodes and try them as articles. But not a periodical or magazine would bite. Rejected sheets piled up until he was ashamed to use any more of her money to pay for stamps.

"You haven't got accustomed to me yet as a failure," he said with his wry smile when she fingered the pages in disappointment. One day when he said it she turned away her head. He knew then that she had got accustomed, and that, too, hurt. In the course of a year and a half he placed two articles in the local press. No one wanted the goods he offered.

But meanwhile he filled in the long days by taking on himself the tasks of the house. He discovered that he could cook, and when she came home the fire was glowing and her slippers were warm.

"You spoil me, don't you," she said, "doing all this for me." He might, he thought then, have made a pretty speech. The occasion offered. But he said, "One must protect oneself." Yes, he thought passionately, from annihilation, from the blankness of not being. I warm your slippers to save myself from the pit."

Elizabeth cheerfully changed the subject.

By the end of their fourth year of marriage he had settled into an adjunct to a busy, energetic and useful Elizabeth.

"Your unpaid secretary," he jested once — and shut his lips hard in dismay at what he had said. Unpaid! But Elizabeth didn't seem to have noticed any implication. She quite sincerely meant that the money belonged to them both — an attitude easier for the giver than for the taker.

In these months he worked out a *modus vivendi* for himself. His wretched body had to be humoured — he blessed the fact that he was so much alone, for he could order his day as he required. Morning was his evil time; it was some hours after he rose before he could shake off a lingering nausea and the lassitude that it involved. Often, having seen Elizabeth away, he would lie down again for most of the morning. But afterwards, whistling as his strength gathered, he would tidy the house and prepare Elizabeth's supper. He had a thrawn satisfaction in menial tasks; they were salt and harsh upon a palate that had tasted too long the poisonous sweetness of self-deception.

"Your batman, madam," he would jest to Elizabeth; and once, "Your dear little wife, in fact."

Elizabeth seemed hardly to be aware that the jest was brittle. If Tommy was happy, as he seemed to be, doing the odd jobs about the house, she was very willing for him to do them. She had, however, her own malaise of spirit. If he wasn't to be famous after all, she was too sensible and too generous to bear him a grudge for that. But she was beginning to be aware that she could no longer exorcise his devils, though, as they weren't the same devils that she had dealt with for so long, she didn't always even recognise the breed.

They were not unhappy. There was friendliness between

them and a genuine interest in the work she was doing. But the heart of their life was dry, a mere dust. Something had gone dead between them, or perhaps there never had been a life there. They had broken through to a level of their being where there was only chaos, and by consent they avoided the empty tract and befriended each other where they could. Tommy saw that it had to be accepted as the necessary corollary of accepting her first fey generosity; and he accepted. It was all in fact part of his descent from the cross, a process that he was finding even more exacting than hanging upon it.

5

In the sixth year of their marriage Elizabeth's father died. He died, Mrs Archibald was wont to say, of his trust deed; for when he fell through the trap of his own barn, the day before the roup, his thoughts were not on doors but on the disgrace of being rouped. "But there's nae a living in these small places since the war — not for a man like your father, who liked to put a skin on his work."

Elizabeth saw the roup through, settled her father's affairs and took her mother to live with her. It did not occur to either Elizabeth or her mother that there was any other thing to do. Indeed the £250 a year that had seemed to her family such wealth for a girl to earn, would allow of nothing else. But within a week Tommy knew he was a homeless man. Diligent and self-effacing, Mrs Archibald rose quietly in the early morning and *put to* her hand. "I would think shame to sit with my hands over other in the house where I get my meat," she said. By the end of a week, with her stocky body, plain big face and honest heart, she had broken down the way of life he had painfully built up for himself. She knew her place, the old woman — her daughter's husband was master, be he who he might, and it wasn't seemly for the master to do a woman's work; nor was it seemly to be cleaning firesides in the afternoon. It affronted her traditions to be idle for a moment till the day's tasks were over; after, she would sit with her shank, straight and decent in her plain black dress, and knit him socks as she had done for more than thirty years to her own husband.

"Now laddie, you'll just be taking off your shoe and try this on till I get the set of your foot." So he thrust his toes awkwardly through the unfinished sock.

"It's a grand sock, mither," he said.

"Mebbe a thochtie tighter round the heel," she ruminated.

He had taken to calling her *Mither,* as Elizabeth did, when she came to live in their house; and he had pictured himself being kind to the stricken old body and paying her attentions. But it was she who paid them to him; and he accepted, though his heart girned at the need. Always the one to take! He mooned out and in, his occupation gone, and his security. The smell of cooking in the morning hours nauseated him, and Mrs Archibald must have her broth at noon. "An honest drop of broth and a tattie — you can't go wrong with a tattie. It'll do you more good than that wabble of milk. You try the broth, laddie."

Elizabeth was busier than ever. Often she wouldn't be home till late in the evening. Her eyes sparkled, her wits were clean and clear. She was on three committees — an incisive speaker, forcible and fearless, in love with her own sense of power. It was a poor substitute for the sweet drunkenness of saving a man from devils, but it served. In her heart she couldn't quite forgive Tommy for not needing her; she had been divine and now was common clay and without knowing it she despised him, just a little, for having settled so easily into his menial role. He knew she despised him, though she didn't know it herself; and he accepted that too. Hadn't he been telling her for a while that he was a small creature?

One afternoon Mrs Archibald, at her shank by the fire, said, "What needs you go up to the bedroom in the cold to your writing? I'll not say a cheep, I'll be as mum's pussie. Stay you here in the warm."

"I wasn't writing," Tommy answered.

"Oh …And is the book near written?"

Tommy had hated few things in his life as much as he hated saying to his mother-in-law, "The book's not going to be written."

"Oh," said the sharp old lady again, "that's the way o't. I wondered what ailed Bet at you. So you'll be needing a job now." And she looked at her son-in-law over the top of her knitting.

"Not very many of them going," said Tommy.

"Hmph," said Mrs Archibald, screwing up one side of her nose, "them that wants to work'll find work."

"Ask Bet the statistics for the unemployed," suggested Tommy. And he went out into the rain. He supposed he had better start the hunt a second time. He wished, though, that his body didn't take so long to limber up to each new day, as though, once sunk in sleep, it settled too far down into the immobility of the inanimate world to be recalled without pain. On the first morning they were left together in the house, his mother-in-law had appeared suddenly in his bedroom with brush and dustpan. "Are you ill?" she had asked, regarding him as he lay on the unmade bed, clad in old slacks and sweater, waiting for the pain to subside and the process of life to re-establish itself in his flesh. "Devil an ill," he had said. "You put that brush away." But she had made the bed and swept the floor. Caught between the upper and the nether millstones of these two capable women, Elizabeth and her mother, he was like to be crushed to powder. Better, perhaps, escape.

In the fourth week, thanks to a man he had known in his

newspaper days, he found work; and wondered what Elizabeth would say to the kind of it; he had engaged himself to go from door to door selling silk stockings.

"That trash," said Elizabeth's mother, exposing an inch or two of her thick strong cashmere. "In my young days we had two pair of hand-woven woollen ones, pair and pair about, to last the year. A young whippertisnappet tried to sell me yon silk things, and me at the farm. A lot o' use they'd be and me sprawlochin' in ower the snow. 'Na, na, ma man,' I said to him, 'My legs is like my wark.' You'd need some mair power at the gab, laddie, for that job. Some o' the weemen'll need a lot o' priggin."

"You won't like it, Tommy," was all that Elizabeth would say; but her eyes were anxious.

"I'll see life," he answered.

He didn't like it, as he had known when he took the commission. He had shut his own door too often behind young men trying to sell him things he either needed nor wanted, not to know that such a pursuit can rot a man's integrity. And he did see life — or some aspects of it that, living as he had been almost as a recluse, he had forgotten: the small discourtesies and meannesses that quite decent people will mete out to the unsuccessful. These things didn't seem worth recounting at home.

One day he said, "I called on a relation of yours to-day — a Mrs Taylor."

"Oh," said Elizabeth. "Christina. Did she know you? She was at our wedding."

"So she told me. She even told me what I looked like — a scarecrow then, an' fient a muckle better are ye now."

"Cat," snorted Elizabeth. "She should have seen you a year ago. I had you looking quite respectable then."

"Anyway, she bought my stockings."

"And real snod she'll look in them," said Mrs Archibald unexpectedly. "Christina has a handsome leg. Did she give you tea?"

Elizabeth in her instructed part knew enough not to be ashamed though her husband peddled goods at her cousin's door; but part of Elizabeth was still tribal, and she was ashamed. The incident spurred her to a project that had been in her mind for some time. Her work at the mill had expanded — why shouldn't the owners afford her some assistance? What Tommy had been doing unofficially he might as well do with official sanction and a wage. She asked for a part-time assistant and suggested that the assistant might be her husband. But the Junior Partner had ideas of his own on welfare and they weren't Elizabeth's ideas; an undercurrent of hostility ran between them. He spoked her neatly, conceded an assistant, but produced his own candidate. "A soft Moll, to do as he wants," thought Elizabeth, her temper rising. She wasn't accustomed to rebuffs and it rankled; and though she hadn't meant to let Tommy know, the tale burst from her and he comforted her.

For himself, he wasn't sorry. He could never have kept hidden from her the misery of his flesh. As it was, he couldn't peddle fast enough. He had already been warned that if his sales weren't better he could go. This brutal, bullying, shoving commercial world had no use for the weak. But he wasn't giving in without a fight. The body could be flogged.

He collapsed in the street one morning, and was taken to hospital with a bloody head.

6

When they told him that he was to die, "All right, don't let my wife know," he had said; and now he lay in the hospital ward and wondered just why he had said it. It wasn't to spare Elizabeth, Elizabeth wouldn't want to be spared. She wanted always to be in at the death.

The one thing he was quite sure of was that he didn't want to die; and that surprised him a little. In these last futile months he had sometimes thought it a pity he hadn't died in Germany. But now as he lay helpless he realised that he had liked these months; there was something cathartic about them. They had gritted harshly on his tongue, but their tart flavour wasn't bad — was definitely good. He had an odd feeling as though he had just begun to live. Was that what the imminence of death did to a man, sharpened his awareness of the savour of living? Elizabeth's angry eyes — that was something to remember. He knew well enough that she hadn't been angry on his behalf, he had no illusions about that; she had been angry over her own humiliation and the threatened interference with her work — he would have been her soft Moll as the new girl would be the Junior Partner's. But God, he liked her fierce.

And then they came and told him that in six months he would be dead.

"Are you under a doctor?" they had asked. Two of them being over his bed at the time, "Seems obvious," he had drawled; but he knew they were not referring to his battered brow.

The doctors were good fellows. They had been, like himself, in the war. One of them had even heard the story of the boys who were strung up by the wrists. To Tommy it seemed far away now, and not very important, but he told them about it, unemotionally, because they asked.

"They say they're doing things like that again," said one of them, "to their political opponents. Messing up the body to destroy the mind."

To destroy the mind, thought Tommy. They had messed his body, right enough, but at least it was without intention. They must be acquitted of that. They weren't to know that a boy, making roads in the Courland forest, who filled his belly with every edible blade and berry he could find, would lodge a fungus in his liver that was eating him now, remorselessly and with all the slow circumstance of indignity. And Tommy came back to the question of why, when after weeks of patient work upon his body they had told him they could not save it from destruction, he had said, instantly and without knowing he was to say it, "Don't tell my wife."

What was craven in him cried out for her comfort, but an obstinacy deeper than his conscious self rose up and confounded him. If he yielded to her now, she could give without stint, flooding him with succour; and he knew that if he let himself yield he would take the succour and love her for it; and that would dissolve, not solve, the problem between them. So, he must wrestle with this alone. He was going to die, and he would die frustrated, impotent and negative. He could hate Elizabeth for her dominant vitality. He had been swept up by her to believe for a day that he could actually do what in his heart he'd always known was merely a dream. If the book could ever have been written, it would have been written before he met Elizabeth; so all he had taken from her he had taken falsely, and now it seemed he was doomed to take and take and give nothing in return. He couldn't die like that. Dying is a lonely task; a man may not have another with him, but he must have himself.

Tommy had at last tracked himself to his darkest lair. He had taken Elizabeth's bounty from a cowardly distaste for common living. Her folk had been right — he had no guts. But to his surprise he faced it without the sick self-contempt he had felt before. It was as though a poison had been expelled from his body. He was small, mean, a nobody, but darkly he understood that he had got through, his feet were on rock. He was a nobody, yet he was somebody, and not the man that had married Elizabeth, who was more than half her own creation. He himself would be the man that died.

He was helped in his determination to stand alone by the small circumstance that his doctors believed they could get him even now a disablement pension. It was impossible to prove that the fungus which was eating out his life had actually entered his body in Germany — there were other things to account for his state of health, an old gastric ulcer, the whole gut in bad condition — but it seemed probable that in time the application would go through. "You'll probably be dead first, my lad," they said, though not to him. The pension was a recognition of himself as an individual, not as an appendage to Elizabeth, and it lent him a little spurious dignity.

Elizabeth was more vigorous than ever. She couldn't be crestfallen for long, her blood was up, and she was blandly blocking the attempts of the new girl to remodel her work. She was fighting gay. The stimulant of her opposition suited her; her work had never been livelier nor her heart more eager. But she wanted Tommy back; he was an extension of her personality that she sorely missed.

The pension hadn't come; they offered to send him to a Military Hospital. "For keeps?" asked Tommy. "You're a hospital case, you know — you'll need expert care now." A raging tumult of life tore at Tommy. He wouldn't be shut up to die. And before he died Elizabeth had to recognise him. To have possessed himself, that was something; but to meet her, self-possessed, not possessed of her, in the farthest reach of their nature, that would be worth living for; or dying for. He, too, grew fighting gay. Before he died, Elizabeth must meet him; not smother him in love. Still pensionless, he let himself be taken home.

7

Tommy, however, had not measured his own weakness. When he tried to rise, he retched in agonising spasms. As his malady grew on him, his dependence also grew; and it was his mother-in-law on whom the burden fell. Her plain realism was medicinal to him. Matter-of-fact and unemotional, she took one service with another, but said, "They haven't done you much good that I can see at that hospital." Tommy pondered the situation. It wasn't only death one had to reckon with, it was dying. He had to be a taker still, it seemed. He realised that he could not take this service from his mother-in-law unless she knew what she was giving; and one day he told her.

Mrs Archibald was quite unprepared for the revelation, and it moved her deeply. She went away but came back after an hour to say, "You'll need to tell her." He shook his head. Implacably experienced, the old woman went on, "It's not the things you think in the riggin' o' the night that you maun go by. She took you for better or for worse, and them that the marriage law binds canna keep a double tongue in their mouth." He shook his head again and she went away.

"Come back, mither," he called after her; and when she came he said, "There's a hospital that'll take me in. Plenty of the lads there still that have been there ever since the war."

She looked doubtfully. "if there's things you need done for you that I can't do — but so long as I can do it, you don't need to go away. Do you want to go?"

"Like hell I do," he said. "It's three hundred miles away."

"But she's got to be told," said Mrs Archibald firmly. "If it were just a common sore belly, well and good. But I can't take the responsibility for this."

"I'll think about it," Tommy promised. After she had gone he lay a long time looking at the line of hill from his bedroom window. Leaving that before he was compelled would hurt nearly as much as leaving Elizabeth. He was defeated again, he supposed. He would tell Elizabeth, and she and the old woman would lave on him all that a man could need, except the sense of mastering his destiny. Life burned in his flesh, its clamour in his blood was strong and urgent. He had wanted, oh God, he had wanted, to compel Elizabeth by some other power than his pitiful need. Lying awake in what the old woman had called the riggin' o' the night, he had known a black satisfaction in his solitary contemplation of death. He stood here unassuaged, learning what a man could endure. But if the mind could endure alone, the body plainly couldn't. In the end he told Elizabeth.

Like her mother, Elizabeth was utterly unprepared; and at first her quick optimism refused to believe it. He steadily beat down each proposal and objection till she was convinced that he had told her the truth. Then to his horror she broke completely. Her face was ravaged, like a landslide on a familiar coast. "And you kept it from me? My God, how could you play with me like that?" The salt of her tears was on his mouth.

At dawn, with Elizabeth fallen asleep at last from exhaustion, in his arms, he knew that the price of his doom was hardly yet begun to be reckoned.

8

Yes, to face death alone in the darkness of the night, slowly to inure oneself to contemplate dissolution, that could be borne; but to face death with Elizabeth was terrible. He understood now why he had shrunk from telling her. All was clear to him at last. He loved her, that was all. And now he knew that she loved him in the same primordial way. Nothing they could do, or fail in doing, to each other could make any difference; and far from the sharing of sorrow halving it, it monstrously reduplicated both his pain and hers, like mirrors that reflected each other to infinity. And now it seemed to him that all he had endured was only a preparation for this final pain. That he should be the stronger of the two was simple; he had more practice in endurance.

Mrs Archibald had heard her daughter's dreadful weeping in the night, and knew that the disclosure had been made. To her it was impiety that a wife should not be by her husband's bedside while he died, and she said to her daughter, "Your folk would maybe let you off a while."

Elizabeth drew her brows down and answered, "Likely not. It might be a month, or it might be six." But her brow stayed knitted. Her work was dear to her; besides it was her future, and their livelihood; and she knew well enough that an indefinite leave of absence was improbable. She was too high-handed in her game; if she let go now, the game was lost, and it wasn't only for her own sake that she wanted to win. She believed sincerely that her ideas were worth the fight. Against that she put Tommy. His sunken eyes, emaciated flesh and the still wells of his patience stayed with her. His languorous, slightly drawling voice, in which, now that it was an open secret, he made lewd jests at his own condition, stole her wits away. It never ceased to amaze her that Tommy, who had been fastidious over his body, should find the extremities of its indignity funny. At the end of a week, when she was with her mother, the fire alone to light them, she sat looking at the older woman's stocky upright figure and the calloused hands folded in her lap, and said, "Mither, would it hurt you very much to take the old age pension?"

Mrs Archibald answered, "Were you thinking of not supporting me, then?"

"I've given up my job," Elizabeth replied.

"Eh, lassie," said the older woman anxiously, "how are we to live?"

"Like the robins," said Elizabeth laughing. "There'll be plenty more jobs later on. I've some money banked, and I'll go into debt if need be. And they say Tommy's pension is pretty sure to come."

"Your father," said Mrs Archibald, "had aye a terrible ill will at all that pensions. But he never looked, poor man, to be runted himself. It's to be hoped that where he's gone he has some other thing ado than worry about an auld wife signing her name."

Elizabeth didn't even thank her mother. They weren't of the sort that put things like that into words.

When Tommy was told, he looked a long time at the hill beyond his window.

"Are you glad?" she asked at last.

"*Glad?*" He turned and their eyes met.

"What about that pension I was to have?" he said after a while.

"They say it's coming. Sure Tommy."

He chuckled. "It'll come in time to give the Department all the trouble of cancelling it again. Oh, Bet, won't it be a lovely joke if I actually support you for a bit before I die!" He said it gleefully. Queer! Here were two women sacrificing deep-held inclinations to his need, and he could take it without shame or rancour; as though, weeping that night in his arms, Elizabeth had healed him more deeply than he knew.

"And what about the Junior Partner?" he asked.

Elizabeth said grimly, "He can stew in his own juice."

"Cheer up, Bet. There'll be plenty left for you to set right in the world when I'm gone."

His teasing voice was like a sword in her entrails. Elizabeth couldn't yet jest with death, though, as once before, she had leaped blindfold on the future. She knew that a supreme moment was before her, and to dissipate herself on the busy activities of her old life would be to miss its inwardness. Yet as the days passed she found it was not all bliss to serve him. Her vitality was too buoyant and abounding to be contained in a sickroom. She wanted an activity of mind and body that he was not able to endure. The old woman, except for his physical needs, had left him alone, and he had the habit of lonely reverie. But Elizabeth wanted to give him all the richness of life into his remaining hours. She didn't yet understand — perhaps, he reflected soberly, never would — that all the richness of life could be felt in merely being. His passivity was not vacant. It was full with the miracle, eternally renewed, of being. He could never get enough of the single wonder of life. Elizabeth had had herself taught all that she would require to do for the care of his body. She spent herself in devising ways to interest his mind. But she could never quite enter his stillness. How strange it was, he brooded. She had made him free of this still centre of his being, yet she could not herself come into it.

Well, perhaps this was the meaning of marriage vows — to accept the whole of another person, repudiating nothing. No picking and choosing. No nibbling and passing on. As Bet had to accept him in his weakness and incompetence, and in this going from her into the place of his own mind.

Perhaps it was only bodily weakness that gave him this clear quiescence. Sickness then could be an exquisite? He had never imagined, never dreamed, so overmastering a sense of wonder. God, how he loved this life — loved it so much that leaving it ceased to matter; each moment so full, so rounded and complete that while he lived it he wanted nothing else. It was astounding to have no regrets at all, neither for the frustrated past nor because there was no future. As for after death — that wasn't worth considering. There might be something, or there might not. He didn't much mind, for already he had known a life that was eternal and indestructible.

Elizabeth said to him one day, "Tommy, I wish you could write that book now. You know so much."

"Still dreaming of fame, Bet?"

"Not fame. But I did want you to be a big man, Tommy."

He laughed and said, "Just a poor devil without any guts." And his eyes met hers in absolute content.

Elizabeth mended the fire and heard the laugh. It was a laugh without bitterness, a mocking and tender laugh that accepted and encompassed all men's follies and all their aspirations. He is already detached from life or he could not be so happy — it isn't natural, it isn't right, she thought, for to her there was no completion, she was young and vital, she had much living yet to accomplish, and she felt inadequate, an unpractised soul that had stumbled as yet only a few steps and must wander on for a long way. So she mended the fire very slowly, knowing that when she dared to turn, his eyes would find hers with the same fullness of content. Oh, God, she thought, how am I to bear it?

PART II

The Deeside Field writings

The Colours of Deeside

The obvious things — purple heather, grey rock, golden whin — have their importance. They provide mass; pageant effects; breadth and substance in their landscape that can etherialise itself. This, however, is hardly true of the grey. When I hear strangers call our country grey, I do not, necessarily contradict; for if grey is the universal solvent, melting all colours into itself, looking will resolve them back. Our grey land, our grey skies, hold poised within them a thousand shades of colour. The eye finds them with delight; and finds them best not in bright sunshine, which makes colour shallow, but in the cool, clear grey that is yet not cold enough to harden them. The changing of colour values under changing lights is one of the loveliest elements in the beauty of our countryside.

Blue

For the most part our blues are cool — slate-blue, steel-blue, ink-blue, ice-blue, milk-blue. The hot mauves and heliotropes of rainy land in the west are absent. Here, rain in the offing, the land grows navy-blue. Corries take on the depth of gentian, shadowed with hyacinth and violet. But the most characteristic blue of Deeside space and distance is one that I find it hard to name. It is azure thinned out till all its vivid intensity is gone, but not the purity of its colour: beaten to a transparency of itself, but still itself. At every time of year there are days when the distant hills have this clear thin blueness. On other days they are soft lavender; opal; or edged with a hard line of china-blue that means rain to come.

It is predominantly a blue landscape, partly because every-where one can have long views (yet nearby things can be blue too — massed firs, July corn) and the blues have a quality which I have never seen, even in mountain country of extreme beauty, outside Scotland. The colour itself seems to have body; to be substance. It lies like the bloom on a plum, or the pile of plush. Sometimes in a hill hollow it would seem to have its own existence, apart from both earth and sky. The result is to give the landscape depth and at least the illusion of significance. The 'significance' may be reducible to latitude, the lines on which the country is built, and the amount of moisture in the atmosphere: but then we have it on good authority that three notes combined together make a star.

The blue of the sky may be sky-blue; or duck-blue, turquoise or milk or ink (see list above). Water may be like speedwell; or steel or ink (see list above). Atmospherics apart, earth, sky and water being disposed of, the blues are small and private. Of flowers, lupins make the boldest splash, the harebells are tiny but a multitude, they mist the waysides with transparency of blue. So are the violets: sometimes in a June field they lie like pools of water. In the higher country, the dark, serene blue of milkwort; speedwell everywhere — on Ben MacDhui and on Lochnagar a patch of the lovely Alpine Veronica; bland blaeber-ries; and on cottage walls the opaque beady blue of tropaeolum fruits. Birds' eggs, the sheen on the plumage, patches of feathers

— jay, kingfisher, bullfinch, chaffinch, tit — dragonflies, the vivid and definite blue of the small blue butterflies. The frailest blues are woodsmoke and the shadows cast on snow. The most blazing blue is vetch: it runs over field-ends and roadsides like a flame of incandescent mauve. No other colour, not even the orange-reds of autumn, has such intensity.

The Hot Colours

The burning and flaming colours are so ostentatiously a part of autumn that a patch of red on the landscape at any other season sends one straight to find its cause. Even the sky might seem to keep its highest brightness for the late months — November sunset and December sunrise, the harvest moon, the smouldering red in the Aurora. Perhaps this is partly why those fields of moss campion and mountain azalea on the high plateau of the Cairngorms fill one each summer with the same astounded thrill. I have never grown accustomed to their extent and intensity. Each year they are more astonishing than I expected them to be.

Yet in plain fact there is no time of the Deeside year when red may not be found in the natural world: while warm browns, yellows, oranges, flame and the hotter tints of purple are always there.

In tree life — bark, for instance. Consider the deep rosewood beauty of the fir, the glowing purple of the birches. I have seen a wood of birches hang on a hillside in April like the bloom of heather. And when the sap rises in spring, how trunks and boughs and smallest twigs light up! Willows are golden-limbed, elms grow ruddy, a yellow flame runs over the larches. And as buds break on the trees, the eye goes seeking the golden-tan of the beech bud-sheaths, the blood hues of the sycamore (even the young leaves bursting from these burning buds are red like mahogany), the purpling of the whole canopy of the elm as it crumbles into flower (on a young tree I have seen the elm blossom so deep a rose as the sun took it that it might have been an almond). The heart of the wood has fire too. Watch a paling made of quartered fir-trunks after a good soaking of rain. In the grain of the wood is a red warmth. I must confess to thinking the pink tassels of larch and of hazel, more obvious and showy, less lovely than these other flushings of colour in the spring trees.

Grasses, both stalk and flower, have heat. Their ripeness is a pinky russet. Where woods have been felled, the next summer there will be an astonishing growth of flowering grasses that in July are like a knee-deep foam. One seems to be walking through a rosy cloud. Burnished by the sun, they stay pink through the autumn into winter. On unused lands in winter tracts of grass stalks glow with red. Rain deepens the colour, and when they have lain under snow and are released it is deeper still, though never so deep and rare as I have seen a patch of rusty ferns in the mountains, released from its snow cover only in June, with the croziers uncurling on a bed of last year's fronds so red that the colour was like a shout. A field of June grass may be warmly under-run with the little sorrel, whose leaves will later take such rich blood tones.

Red field flowers do not touch the intensity of colouring of buds, leaves, stalks and fruits — cuckoo pint, wild roses, foxgloves, the thistle with its 'scrunts o' blooms'. Ragged robin and rosebay in mass are the most vivid. It is not poppy country. Sundew's brilliance is of leaf and all. There remains Dinnet Moor. Is there anywhere else a blast of red like it; so large a tract of bell-heather, so generously spaced, thrown up to the sun in such a gorgeous abandon? It makes the ling look sober, and sobriety is an odd word to use of ling. But the ling is the lovelier, in so far as gorgeousness is inferior to radiance.

The cryptograms, a small people but numerous, the outcastes of the plant world because they bear no fruits, have a brilliant beauty of their own. What exquisite spore-cups and trumpets, what splashing scarlets! Once one has learned to detect their delicate forms in moorland and wood, on dyke and open hill, one watches ever after for their presence.

But when all is said, autumn has the best of it with the burning colours. Lovely as our hills are in August, in early October they are far more brilliant. Vermilion, scarlet, bloodred, crimson, rose; rust and bronze and gold — mosses, blaeberry leaves, bracken (and that lovely curse), birches, rowans — they blend and separate and merge again. Humble things that have no look in summer flame into beauty after their flowering is over — the tiny tormentil, both leaf and stalk, glows like blood; self-heal drops its rather stolid purple and takes on a deep red-brown, in its tiers of winged seed-pods set tightly round the stalk, like fuzzy red bumble-bees in the grass.

For the most flaming glory of autumn colour on Deeside, both in variety and in close-packed intensity, one should go to those undulating heights from the Shooting Greens down to Potarch and over the river to Sluie Hill; or across the site of the Loch of Leys to the slopes of the Hill of Fare. Every sort of berry, leaf and stem, grass and moss and fern, seems to be there — rowan and hip and haw, bog asphodel, bracken and birch and bramble leaf. A different glory is the red-gold of massed beeches at Countesswells and on the bend of the river at Culter. They, of course, provide one of the richest bits of winter colour, in the deep drifts of fallen leaves that glow far in within the woods. Beech bud-sheaths, blown in tide-mark lines along the edge of the roads, give a glow of brightness to the dusty roads of May.

Massed golds, apart from autumn leaves, are a goodly part of our colour wealth. Broom, whin — and how they deepen in intensity with dusk! The cooler yellow of the prosaic patches of kail seed and turnip seed. Charlock and ragwort, pests but comely. The lesser celandine, marsh marigolds, dandelions. The clear pure gold of oats, peach red on the ripe stalks, the brown of barley. A silken primrose in the sky, chilling to aquamarine. Or bronze-gold, in winter, welling over half the west.

Among the sky colours the rainbow, I suppose, must have mention. But I dislike rainbows. Their smug regularity annoys me: though rainbow colouring, in spray, on broken edges of cloud, in the broch around the moon, is beautiful. Sunrise or sunset colouring caught on the earth itself can surprise — solid material things seem to change their nature: I have watched many a time that very cold grey building, Blairs College, glow deep rose for half an hour at a time in the reflected sunset. Bare fields set well up to the north-west seem to be not soil but some ruddy growth. And when this reflected light is on bell-heather, the effect is like fire. Mortlich from Aboyne, better still the tumble of low heights between Tarland and the Dee as seen from Dinnet Moor, blaze luridly upon the July nights.

The wink of outdoor fire itself is an integral part of the country's life — heather fires, fires of weeds and potato shaws, whin fires. And the ruddy faces, the weather-tanned necks and arms, the red hair and the freckles of the folk themselves — how good they are, how vital and vigorous! And the red cows and horses, the redbreasts and redshanks, red ants and red Admirals, red spiders and red squirrels, red deer and red fox — the hand-somest brush I have ever seen was on the slopes above Glen Derry. Vivid and solid, combs and wattles and bills. Vivid and aerial, crests and breasts. Exciting in their rarity, the waxwing (I have seen only one, on Glen Gairn) and the Golden Eagle, of whom my loveliest vision occurred high above the Pools, where, glinting in the sun, he soared serenely out from below my feet on the Braeriach crag. Sinister brightness — the zigzag of the adder. I have met him most frequently on the Feugh and the Quoich.

The earth itself has warmth of colour. A drift of water-washed pebbles seems grey: look into it, and numbers of the stones are rosy pink. Felspar colours them as it colours 'sandy' sands. And through the grey stone break veins of rose-red porphyry: one can see them here and there about the bed of the streams — at Potarch, at the Brig of Feugh. Decomposed felspar and oxides of iron make the naked soil red brown.

Green

Chlorophyll, that odd substance, dominates but does not quite monopolise this act. But even if it were a sole agent, the Act would be dramatic, so subtle in alteration, so infinite in tone, are the greens of growth, according to the texture and nature of the material in which the chlorophyll is working. From the all-but-black of an ancient pine to the all-but-white of just opening hornbeam leaves, the shades of green are literally countless: between integer and integer on the colour scale one requires all the resources of repeating decimals. Grass-green: a colour intolerable in anything but grass, vulgar, crude; but in grass — what shade indeed is it? Three lawns in three adjacent gardens may be of quite different tints, and every one of the three will alter with seasons and weathers. As for a 'girse park' - near, as one stands in it, afar, part of a slope or curving boss, at dawn and at noon, wet, sun-scorched, with its vagrancy of flowers, its underlying soil, its tilt and exposure, shut in by dykes or shadowed by forest, or widening out through open palings to further fields — who is to say what colour a grass field really is? Moss-green: another intolerable shade in the draper's shop. But if I go into a wood, in five minutes I have five different green mosses in my hand. And think of the greens of stalk and calyx and bud-sheath, of the veining in leaves and petals, of trees standing singly with the light in them and trees massed into forest; of marshland and waterweed and the lurid pond-scum; of the green flowers — the rare muscatel, lady's mantle — of ferns and the trivial tender white-green toadstools; of greens in juxtaposition — fresh tips of the spruce against the sombre elder foliage, larch and Scots fir in April, the upper and under side of wild raspberry leaves played in by the wind; of any tree as it follows the cycle of its year, from the first flush of sap in the stem to its withdrawal from the finished leaves. The birch, for instance — from its February purple to its golden fall, bark, twig, sprinkled buds, catkins, early and late leaf — the birch by itself is a study in colour that provides endless delight.

Yet bountiful as she is in greens, Deeside is not a green land. I think this is partly because of the trick distances have (even green distances) of turning blue; and partly because long views almost invariably end in heather: because, too, the width of the land gives one such a sweep of sky. So blue and brown are the colours I should choose as of the very nature of this country. This, however, I know may be a personal finding. Colour is notoriously subjective. So if I see blue and brown as the colours that express the very identity of Deeside, it may only be, first, because I like summer least of the seasons; and second, because my eyes being normally long-sighted, I look often at distances.

Although I have insisted on the variety of greens in plant life, yet it must be said that where chlorophyll enters into the making, the greens have a recognisable common quality, and there are certain shades of the colour never to be found in plants; metallic greens, for instance, such as verdigris; or jade; or the bright pure green of glacier water. These beautiful colours can, however, be seen generously on Deeside, but in the sky. The green skies of evening — of still and gleaming evenings

— have that quality. Or chrysophase, if one takes the trouble to look at it in a geological museum, is seen to be a just image for the green sky: so that the new heaven and new earth of the Vision promise to be recognisably like our own.

Water also in the high mountains can be green, and not from any vegetable alloy. In the high country too there are exquisite tiny beetles, with wing-cases like green enamel: green dragon-flies, sleek pale caterpillars in gardens: lovely bands of dark soft green on the wild duck's neck: veinings of green in the wings of the white cabbage butterfly. There are lusty fellows of bottle-green that we do not seem, on the analogy of the blue-bottle, to call greenbottles; but that abhorrent and ubiquitous creature, the aphis, does not deserve so good a name as the green fly.

Cats' eyes are green. And are the eyes of the wild creatures, glimpsed suddenly in the dark of woodland, green also; or do they seem so? Is it a green of some strange void one sees, watergreen, the glint of an outer light reflected or of an inner light unveiled?

White

Whiteness is in snow, and in massed cumuli. The higher reaches keep their snow for weeks, or months, or aeons. In 1934 only the snow patch of the Garbh Corrie stayed the course. So only it can now claim to be eternal snow; but the whiteness of snow, as of shining clouds, is integral to the colour history of this countryside. Otherwise pure white is to be found only in small touches — very delicately in certain wild flowers, the stitchworts, trientalis starring the June woods (a flower altogether of northerly parts) hawthorn, gowans, gean: a grove of gean gives the biggest stretch of pure white (apart from snow and sky) unless it be a daisied or a gowaned field. In the mountains, white is in the cotton-grass, the brief bloom of the cloud-berry, an outcrop of milky quartz (there is one of gleaming whiteness on the summit of Morrone) the wheatear's cheeky rump, ptarmigans' wings (with their line of silver-black along each feather), white hares vanishing up a hillside like streaks of smoke.

The other smoke, of blown spray from waterfalls, is rarer here than in counties like Argyll, or abrupter slopes; though Corriemulzie and the Linn and the Chest have the rich whiteness of broken water; and the young Dee plunging over its precipice beneath the Wells can be seen as a white streak from a long way off.

Close mists can be ghostly white. Sudden showers of sleet in April, slanting before a wind, move like sheeted hosts. Hoar frost on bramble leaves and grey dyke stones bristles white like a living pelt. On a September morning an acre of whin will gleam softly white from the moisture caught in its innumerable veils of spider web. There is a dead whiteness of sky that is the most lifeless thing I know.

There are white cows and horses, though the red and brown and black are more our own; hens by the hundred, and ducks; lambs (doubtfully); sheep are grey (or nowadays a virulent yellow, like the lusher sort of Finnan haddie). The 'white moths glimmering through the dusk' are a deception: dusk whitens them to our gullible eyes.

White wings, white bands, white cross-bars, make plumage endlessly enticing. The dipper's white dicky is a joy. The lovely tern is rare, oyster-catchers impossible to miss. Gulls are far and away the commonest of the white birds, wheeling and flashing over the river from the sea to the far uplands. White swallows nested for years in the eaves of the gamekeeper's cottage at the Bridge of Dye.

White fruits, the snowberry; white tails, the rabbit and the deer; white noses, the plough-horses; white wings, dandelion and thistle seeds; white eggs, the ant; white nests, the spider; white armour, the cuckoo-spit; white insides (and how white) the snail — but we have to go to a laboratory to see that, so it doesn't count.

Black

Absolute black is rare. One finds it in small details — ash buds, black spots on decaying sycamore leaves, the shapely shining seed heads of myrrh, crowberries, brambles, elder berries, the heart of cornel, satin slugs, the small chimney-sweeper moth that flits by day in thin birch woods on the edge of heather, the hooves of the roe. Ripe broom pods (coal-black) have the faintest grey down along the edges; the whin pod is covered completely by down, and is never truly black.

Near-black are the bursting ash-flowers (darkest grape) wood rush (perhaps bullrushes) and the humble carl-doddy.

Charred heather and whin make the most extensive patches of true black, though black as a tone value rather than a colour may sweep earth and sky. Midnight in the open is rarely black; under spruce trees the blackness is solid, palpable. By day, there is a storm-black without blue in it, cindery, neither shadowed nor lustred, the hue of extinction.

Some shadows (but not nearly all) are black. So are some waters. So is sodden heather. So may sodden, leafless trees appear — it depends on how one stands in relation to the striking of light. If one faces the light, the trees are black; if one's back is to it, astonishing colours will glow from the sodden boughs, mahogany and rose. Sodden earth, the soil itself, rarely looks black: there is too much red in it. A thick fir-wood against the evening sky is black like velvet.

Ripe black seeds are a myriad; so are black stamens; so are flies; and crows. Flocks of starlings in the sky look black, but on

51

the ground are iridescent. A host of birds have notable black markings. Rook and raven darken the mind by their swarthiness, but the blackbird's black is cheerful. The black of a bunch of cows in a field is smooth as Iodex ointment. Best of all, to a native of the valley — the black faces of sheep.

The Colour of Water

The water of the valley, being swift-flowing, is clear. Brown, even Hopkins' lovely "horse-back brown" may be seen after flooding, but is not the common colour of the hill burns. I have seen the Crathes burn look very brown, and the Crynoch Burn. The Dee itself below the Pools, is of a crystal clearness that catches the breath. Loch A'an may be clearer, I am not quite sure. Perhaps it is only that the clarity there is intensified by sheer mass. Both must be among the whitest waters in the world. Green water, too, is characteristic, an astonishing, transparent green. Of the Green Lochs of the Cairngorms, three lie towards the Dee basin, and among the mountain tributary streams several are green. The greenest is the Quoich. It is birch-leaf green in its shallows, glass-green in the deeper pools.

The blackest water is Loch Kandar, though I know some uncelebrated pools, deep in woods, that are almost as black. The river itself can be sapphire, but when one bends over and looks in, its jewel quality may be quite gone. I have seen a full river, after flooding, speedwell blue from a short way off, whose curves, when one looked close, welled over in murky blood-hues (this in noon light) the edges of the water at the further bank took the light in a fringing of heliotrope.

Man's Colours

Hoses, conveyances, implements, bridges, boundaries. The grey stone dykes, thanks to the rounded contours of the weathered stone seem almost a natural feature of the country. So do old stone bridges, lovely and shapely, like the Bridge of Dye, the old Bridge of Invercauld, and that simple, plain but perfectly poised drystone bridge at Easter Ord, built with his own hands by the brother of my great-grandmother. Concrete as a bridge material is only arriving on the Dee. It lends itself to beautiful line, that can be shaped to the country: its problem where colour is concerned lies in its smooth uniformity of surface, that does not break the light; though moulding and stepping in the concrete itself can be used to modify this. The new bridge at Altries has a plainness of white that at present is staring.

The suspension bridge raises the question of paint. White, the usual choice, emphasises the form of the structure, which, by its very nature, cannot have the dignity and seemliness of stone. The green that has recently replace the white of the Shakin' Brig has the sad disadvantage of agreeing with the vegetable greens around it only on occasion. The same is true of various poles, posts and boxes, which the multiple public services of modern life demand about our roads. To paint these green is excellent in idea, but in practice it seems to be difficult to find a green paint that really harmonises with the greens of vegetation. Black in the green might give too sombre a shade, but it would merge better into the myriad tones of the natural greens. (Only, to be inconspicuous is not an ambition of modern life.)

Petrol pumps flaunt for the same reason as the peacock and the peony; and their flaunting is not always disagreeable. There is an effective grouping at one spot of burnt orange, yellow and scarlet. (A Scottish county that is not Aberdeen, however, paints all its petrol pumps a pleasant green.) Tin advertisements are a worse offence than filling stations. The line between gaiety and gaudiness in paint is not always easy to distinguish. Vivid blues and reds on cartwheels and ploughshares are happy, but there has been of late a fashion for doors and windows of a peculiarly hard and vapid blue, or a red like raw fresh liver, that are not happy. Some lovely things can be done about the trimmings of homesteads and gardens (sheds, gates, palings) with combinations of different paints — green and soft primrose, for instance; or black and a dull rust-red, which give the appurtenance of one Deeside garden an unusual elegance.

For buildings, grey granite is, of course, right. So is white or drab harling: the roughcast catches shadows and merges into the living pattern of colour as a painted surface cannot. Slates and thatch belong. Old mellow red tiles — brown-red, autumn coloured — can be very beautiful; there are old cottages dotted here and there, often by the river, whose colour is sure and true. But the pink of asbestos roofing, which is one of the most empty colours I know, is like a postage stamp stuck on to a watercolour. One good red-tiled cottage at a certain bend on the river has recently added to itself a shapely tarred wooden shed, spoiled, alas, by pink asbestos. A farm on a lovely curving sweep of upland has a new steading (I am sure by its size a most hygienic and commodious steading) the rather blatant red of which leaps out at the eye from miles around. Will the landscape absorb it? Will it absorb the "butcher-coloured scum of little houses" that is replacing the tall, narrow grey houses of the past? How perfectly the grey houses grow from the land one can see from Kingcausie or Crathes Castle, or Birss, which, though largely a modern reconstruction, rises up against its hillside as though it had been there for ever; or the church spires of Tarland and Lumphanan, that, from whatever angle one approaches, soar sweetly up in perfect accord with the country around.

It is, however, to be noted that not all apparently grey spires, bridges and what-not are of grey stone: they may be the warm variety, lichened and weathered. Just as the tumbled outcrop of rock on the peak of Mount Keen, seen from even a short distance off, appears grey but is in reality pink, so with Aboyne Church and Ballater Bridge. Indeed, all along that portion of valley –Kincardine, O'Neill, Aboyne, Dinnet — the building stone is the warm-coloured kind, which is probably why the pleasantest of all Deeside red-roofed buildings are thereabout. There is, too, a practical custom of using in houses, walls, road metalling, stones of all the varieties that are at hand — granites, porphyries, schists, white-grey, blue-grey, pink. A pit in a boulder-clay deposit will show them *in situ* (there is one just beyond Ballater, on the south side). One house in Kincardine O'Neill turns to the road a gable-end of particularly pleasant aspect, in which the colours merge so softly that one hardly notes their presence. The result is as natural and right as the grain in wood.

James McGregor and the Downies of Braemar

On the twenty-ninth of December 1960, there died, far from the 'Braes' that were a very part of him, in his daughter's home at Fairburn, James McGregor of Braeview, the highest of the crofts at Tomintoul on Morrone, one of the old Gaelic-speaking Roman Catholic residue of the Braemar folk. Whether he had actually spoken the old tongue as the language of daily experience I am not sure. His mother did, and he loved to roll phrases of it over his tongue, sometimes, one suspects, to mystify and titillate his audience. He was a mystifier of genius. Nothing pleased him more than to draw a listener on, to tease, to tantalize. Some did not like his teasing tongue, finding it too sharp. They did not recognise for what it was a little toss of the head that he had, which belied the stern face and sometimes almost angry voice to which he said the most preposterous things. His quirky mind had an endless delight in the droll and the absurd.

Why I should begin by writing of his drollery I hardly know. His solid worth should come first. He was a man knotted and grained, spare and stringy in his flesh, an insatiable worker. His whole life was lived out on the croft occupied by his forbears, said to be the highest croft in Scotland, sitting to the hill on the Tomintoul corner of Morrone, just below where the Field Club indicator now stands. He made a living from these exposed and stony fields, supplemented by working as ghillie, as gardener, as occasional postman 'up the glen'; but he had other skills, for with his own hands he had built the house to which he brought his bridge when his uncle, his mother and his aunt, the last of the older Downies, still lived in the old house that is now a ruin. He channelled the water from the hill and had water on tap and 'flush' sanitation. He even made his own electricity and wired his house, though the illumination was too meagre to be very useful. Where did he get these skills, he whose schooling was minimal and who had no apprenticeship or training? Working as a labourer with carpenter or builder, he drew in knowledge like breathing. His natural ability was of a very high order. Education and training might have made him a highly successful man; I do not think they would have made him a more interesting one. From his mother's people, the Downies, he took his grit and solid strength of character, yet what of his inheritance came to him from the Gregarach, that dispossessed, wily and wandering clan, fierce in their antagonisms, children of mystery, who is to say? Nimble of wit, caustic of tongue, infinite in his curiosity, picking up knowledge where he needed it, with the acumen that refuses nothing that is to its purposes, into old age he kept a perennial quickness, the quick of life, which could on occasion be disconcerting. He was up on you before you knew it, surprised the very thoughts out of your head. One conversed with him, not merely chatted. There was give and take in all his conversations. No-one stayed in his house but he drew from their stores of knowledge, their peculiar lore. I think none stayed there but learned from him.

My friendship with him began on an April day in the twenties. As it chanced, I had not been in Braemar since the July of 1914 and had not understood that the old croft had seen alterations. I had known it of course in my girlhood, for we never climbed Morrone but we stopped to look at its ancient knobble of glass in one of the windows, to speak to the old people and perhaps be allowed to peep in at the door of the old house ('up-by' as it always was to us after we became habituees of the new cottage lower down) and see the deas, the box-bed, the plate-rack reaching to the roof and gleaming with flowered plates and bowls. This was the home of the Downies, a family who came from Corriemulzie to Tomintoul on Morrone when the then Duke of Fire was stocking his forest with deer. John Downie the grandfather was a mountain guide for many years. John his eldest son married and went as shepherd to Invercauld. Of his other two sons, William after his father's death ran the croft and went to the deer-stalking in the autumn. James helped on the croft and carried on the work of mountain guiding.

On the April day when I first saw the 'doon-by' house, its diminutive size, its compactness, the ingenuity with which it used every fraction of its interior space, its stair that ran up straight and narrow like a ship's companion-way, its gable window, its poised and groomed assurance, stole my heart and for a very long time we went back at least once, often twice a year. Mrs McGregor then and always was the perfect hostess and up-by, still master of the croft but living by himself in the bothy, was old James Downie. I won his friendship the first night by climbing Morrone as soon as I had settled in, and till his death some years later we were fast friends. When I returned from my first Ben MacDhui climb he doffed his bonnet and clasped my hand in a gesture that was pure ceremonial. I was initiate. His tales had a delicious tang — like bog-myrtle or juniper, sharp and good; of ladies climbing Lochnagar in trailing skirts; of the Loch Callater shepherd who had to provide *shalts* for them to ride and who hid in his bothy and wouldn't help to mount the ladies, saying later to Downie, 'I likit fine to see ye settin' them on the shalts'; of Gladstone, a guest at Balmoral and desiring to see the Pools of Dee, but refusing to go the half-mile beyond the Pools that would have led him to the summit of the Pass and the long view over the Spey, and Downie, true hillman, deprived of his view, bearing a grudge for it fifty years after. The last time I saw him he insisted on carrying my bag all the way to the bus and would take no refusal. 'I'll not see you again.' And indeed before I returned he was gone.

But his nephew remained, and with each visit our appreciation of him grew. There was a hard core in him; he was unsparing to himself and to his family, demanding of each their due of labour; but back-breaking toil could not quench his curiosity. He was the most satisfying of listeners. When I went up for a few days by myself, wandering all day alone on the hills, I could tell him on my return all that I had seen and heard. His comments intensified my knowledge.

And how he loved to catch us out in some stupidity — sleeping out without a tent after a blazing day when he warned us (and we wouldn't listen) that there would be ground frost at night — and us creeping in sleepless and shivering to be gleefully mocked for long enough. I can see him still fondling Conny (she was born in Glen Conny), at ease before the kitchen fire and stealing covert and wicked glances at me. 'Did she do it to you then? That bad woman. Poor lass, poor lassie, was that a way to treat my dog?' And suddenly we all three explode with laughter, Conny jumping with short excited barks, and we throw her her ball, and play. But Conny and I are weary and our laughter subsides and we laze, enjoying the fire.

For it is January and this morning Conny, who will not be kept off the hill, has followed me up Morrone. The land is

59

gleaming white, the snow is made up of a million sharp-edged atoms of ice that a furious wind lifts and drives against us. They strike me at knee level but Conny in the eye. She looks pitifully at me, we stop again and again and with the warmth of my bare hands I free her shaggy eyebrows from the ice. I wear ridged rubber boots on which the snow does not cling but her paws are weighted with balls of ice. I hold them in my hands and free them, and say, 'Go home, Conny.' But I can't turn back and she will not. We reach our summit. 'Did she do it to you then, poor beast?' I can hear her master's voice, teasing, affectionate, enjoying its own virtue. But the small hot room is full of friendliness: he knows why Conny and I had to go on. And he listens attentively to my description of the strange columnar structure I have found in the snow near the summit, and of the hunting eagle that flew low up the valley.

I saw him last in the autumn of 1960 when he was a stricken man. The swiftness had gone. Speech and movement were slow and difficult. We were seated by the fire when a niece of Mrs McGregor, who had been up by the top gate, came running down to tell us that a long line of stags was passing across the hillface. We hastened up the slope to the top gate to watch, leaving the old man by the fire. The stags stood out against the sky, then disappeared into a dip. We were about to turn away when they appeared again, taking the next flank of the hill with a perfection of grace. We stayed on, watching. Then I was aware that James McGregor too was with us. He had made his slow painful way up to see again a sight seen a thousand times and still desirable. It is a good last memory.

In the last few years of his tenure the land was let out for grazing. There were no beasts in the byre, no crops in the fields. Probably there will never be so again. Like other marginal land it will not be cultivated. One ponders the fate of the garden he made with such love and skill. In 1927 my friend Agnes Mure

Mackenzie, sleeping in the bedroom with the gable window, woke at dawn to see sixteen stags in the garden. Her presence at the window startled them and they flowed like a wave over the containing wall. Later new ground was broken for the garden and it was fenced securely from deer and rabbit (and padlocked from other marauders in the recent winters and springs that the elderly couple spent at the home of a married daughter) and cleared of moles by John C. Milne, who made a hobby of catching the black velvet fellows while on holiday. Then the high windy land was fed to an astounding fertility. Flowers grew and blossomed — but along with the cultivated flowers there was by the door an exquisite clump of bluebells, their slender stems and delicate inflorescence increasing year by year. And one remembers too the roebuck antlers, the milky quartz, the wind-chiselled pieces of limestone from the limestone streak that runs across Morrone, the shared and twisted stones from the valley of the Ey: all placed with natural rightness. Into the parcel of land — house, fields and garden — was put the genius of this man.

Wild Geese in Glen Callater

A gamekeeper told me once that on the night of every fifteenth of October, the migrating geese descend upon Loch Einach, filling its great hollow with the rushing of their wings. Here are their sleeping quarters as they pause on their journey from the north-west. That is the night, and I must go; he had been there, had seen them coming in their hundreds.

I have never gone there on the fifteenth and do not know if this precision in the date is correct. If it is, it sounds like some ancient earth-magic, the creatures obeying the turning of the earth in its orbit; like Beltane and Yule an immovable rite. Certainly it is in October that one may see the skeins of geese arrowing their way towards the south. I have spent in Glen Einach a whole October day that was punctuated by their harsh alien crying: and here in my garden on Lower Deeside I have heard the honk that always sets me searching the sky for the delicate arrow. I can never see it unmoved. Primeval forces are there, made for a moment visible. One wintry morning a skein passed so close over my head as I stood at my own door, that I could count with ease the individual birds: there were ninety-six of them, one edge of the plough-share more than twice the length of the other.

It was too on an October day (but earlier than the fifteenth) that I watched a skein of geese fly up the Callater valley. I had clambered up to the watershed from which one looks down into Glen Doll, and discovered (what I had not realised in the sheltered valley) that an October gale, bitter and blustering, was raging up from the south. I was buffeted and mishandled and soon dropped down again to the shut-in valley head. It was then that I saw the geese, flying fairly low and on the other side of the water. They made a handsome phalanx, some eighty strong, in perfect formation, steady and straight, with a sharp clean arrow-head.

They passed the point where I was standing and reached the watershed and the wind. Then as I watched, the point of the arrow was blunted, the leading bird swerved to the right, the next two or three bunched together, then a new bird struck out as the leader and the line went on: but only for a moment — the new leader also swerved, the birds bunched, another individual took over the leadership and the line again went on, straight and true. But again the leader swerved and the birds bunched for a moment till yet another flew ahead and the formation righted itself. The birds, however, had had enough. When the fourth leader swung right about each bird wheeled along with her — or was it him? A youngster learning the game? Without disorder, so swiftly that one had hardly seen it happen, they were again in clean sharp formation, back down the valley they had just come up. On the far side of the water, a diaphanous cloud had gathered and the birds flew into it. I strained my eyes to watch them, but they grew fainter and fainter, now a silver point, at last a wraith, a memory of shape — I could not have sworn that I was still seeing them. I do not know where they went, nor at what lonely loch or tarn they alighted, nor how long they were deflected from their proper path. But I cannot forget the ease and purpose in that deflected flight. The birds faded out into the cloud like an embodiment of mystery; they came and they were gone: I have kept them ever since.

The Lupin Island

In my early childhood — and indeed for much longer — one of the rites of early summer was a visit to the Lupin Island. This island lies off the south bank of the Dee, about half way between Ardoe and the Shakin' Brig and in those days it was covered from end to end with blue lupins, carried downstream, it was supposed, by seed throw-outs from Balmoral and Borrowstone. Then at a date I cannot fix, but which was probably about the later twenties, a ferocious spate scalped the island completely. When the water fell, every lupin had been swept away, and not one ever grew again.

Meanwhile the river continued on its wayward course. In time it breached the raised parapet between the bridge and the south road, an immense bank of stones was washed up on the north side, the main current poured on to the south pier instead of between the piers, the bridge became unsafe. Then a bulldozer was set to work on the accumulation of shingle, shifting it across the bed of the river and leaving it piled in an island so that the main current broke upon it, the major part going again between the piers. Two years ago this islet was bare shingle, last year it was flushed with green, in May this year it blazed with lupins. I came on it with startled delight. Time turned back: there, I thought are my old lupins alive again, seeds, roots, miraculously resurrected. My botanical friends sobered me down. This must be a fresh colony, seeds carried downstream finding the empty shingle a perfect place to germinate and lupins enjoying such a habitat, just beyond the reach of the river. The main current, too, washes against the islet, while the old lupin island, still bare of lupins, is now untouched by it. I have discovered, also, half-a-mile upstream from the bridge, two solitary plants growing close against the north bank, undoubtedly water-borne. At the date of writing, autumn 1965, the fate of the bridge is uncertain, but the effort to save it has at least given us again a lupin island.

PART III

Poems

Achiltibuie

Here on this edge of Europe I stand on the edge of being.
Floating on light isle after isle takes wing.
Burning blue are the peaks, rock that is older than thought,
And the sea burns blue — or is it the air between? —
They merge, they take one another upon them.
I have fallen through time and found the enchanted world.
Where all is beginning.
The obstinate rocks
Are a fire of blue, a pulse of power, a beat
In energy, the sea dissolves
And I too melt, am timeless, a pulse of light.

OCTOBER 4TH 1950

69

Next Morning

This morning the rocks are adamant — we knew they were —
Monsters, planting their feet against the gale.
The bright sea is itself, and could be no other,
Sharp and hard, cavorting and lashing its tail.

A world in active mood, knowing the grammar of now,
The present tense, a fierce exultation of act,
No meanings that cannot be shouted, no faith but is based
On the tough, the mendacious intractable splendour of fact.

OCTOBER 5TH 1950

On a still morning

I hear the silence now.
Alive within its heart
Are the sounds that can not be heard
That the ear may not dispart?

As white light gathers all —
The rose and the amethyst,
The ice-green and the copper-green,
The peacock blue and the mist —

So if I bend my ear
To silence, I grow aware
The stir of sounds I have almost heard
That are not quite there.

OCTOBER 6TH 1950

Rhu Coigach

A headland on the Atlantic

Thrusting at me the gaunt rocks cry:
This is the end, there is nothing further to know,
Here is the last foothold, the whelming wave is beyond
There is no more for the mind to undergo.

But the rocks lie: there is negation to undergo
To know oneself blank, blind, worthless, rejected, done,
A stranger in the outwash of a bitter sea.
This too must be apprehended, its savour won.

OCTOBER 1950

Falketind

With cruel beak and one black pinion spread,
Scourging the sky, the Falcon mountain towers,
Fierce to be free of heaven, doomed to be rock,
Type of our own accursed agonizing,
Wrestling with gods for nights that are not ours,
Man's doom prefigured, his absolution wrought.
Through his eyes he is absolved, his climbing feet,
Through the long halt, gazing, the breath caught,
On that black sweep of wing, that lifted head.

The Trees

Forgotten temples in forgotten lands,
Half quarried stone forbidden to achieve
The form some master-thought had asked to leave
Cut on it – and reflected there it stands,
Lichened and frustrate – columns that the sands
Have long since gulfed and cities that the heave
Of earth's cramped body carelessly did thieve
Of fame, and halls both raided and ruined by hands:

All these I thought on – all the dead done world,
Deliberate things and things without desire.
For it was April, and I dared not look
Save furtively upon the trees, that whirled
And fled and followed my path. And one was fire,
One mocked; one melted while I swore she shook.

MAY 5TH 1918

Underground

What passionate tumult tore this black disturbance
Out of the rugged heart of the obstinate rock,
Fixing secure a thousand-age-old shock
Beneath the quiet country's imperturbance,
I have no wit to utter, nor what breath
Blew like a bubble that flees through water this
Chasm in the bowels of earth where dark streams kiss
In guilty dark slant shores they will kiss till death

And never look on: but I give my thanks
Tonight to that antique destructive whim
That so the risen and torrential flood
That else had burst all measure and drowned the banks
And swamped my life, may pour along those grim
And secret caves, and none discern its thud.

MAY 1918

The Dryad

So faunus leaped: and she, caught unaware,
Flung back one wild glance at her tree, and spoke
No word, nor shrieked, but desperately broke
From his embrace; recaptured from the snare
Broke twice, and thrice: the fourth time mute despair
Shackled her limbs. She drooped. But he could cloak
Lust in rare beauty and of the brutal folk
She too was born. She laughed and yielded there.

And after all, why flee? — since not in flight
Is there escape for her from tyrant earth.
Her flickering limbs that flare and flash from sight
Are scarce her own, but through the flickering boughs
Must melt, and she be captive to the mirth,
Snatched by the faun or not, of earth's carouse.

MAY 19TH 1918

76

Arthur's Seat

Early Morning

That summer night a haze of apricot
   Drifted about the spires and houses. Low
   And luminous it hung, and in the glow
The city trembled, like a thing half-wrought
From dreams and wild desire, that ere the thought
    Took substance faded, till it seemed to grow
    Part of the very sky, and none might know
The earth from heaven. Dusk quivered. Dark shook them not.

And we at morning found the city lying,
   And a flash of sea and the mountains-line afar,
   Gathered in awful trance: and watched it broken:
But kept, while earth, indifferent and flying,
   Danced on through heaven like any other star,
   One still rapt secret way of hers for token.

JULY 1ST 1919

77

The Burning Glass

Be not my burning-glass! O love, I fear.
　　The low faint star, blue of the thunder-haze,
　　Blurred water-pools — the beauty of them dismays
My senses, that hold precariously dear
Loveliness that defeats them. Year by year
　　I clutch the radiance by scattered rays,
　　Dreaming till death of one proud fusèd blaze,
The revelation, earth's beauty caught and clear.

And now knowing thee I tremble with fear that thou
　　Utter the secret word that clarifies.
O, I could watch my world blaze up and perish
As price of that dread knowledge! Yet, not now:
　　And be not thou the glass: lest I must cherish
　　More than thyself the word that makes thee wise.

MAY 1921

Union

Dear, I have not kept back, though I made my boast,
Once, to have dark reserves and hidden store
Of mine own intimate self: but now no more
I am afraid to offer the uttermost
And come all naked to thee: yet thou Know'st
Though more, still less of me than e'er before.
Seeing that the giver gives and the gift is o'er.
But when giver and gift are one, to the end thou ow'st.

Ah love, surrender could not be more complete!
But in the very surrender I discover
New intimacies to show to thee my love
And showing, yet newer privacies secrete,
Till ever upon the marge of oneness we hover,
Yet ever, O love, from lonelier travelling meet.

Street Urchins

In dim green summer silence the woodland
    Lay and I with it, through the afternoon;
And the dusk of pine and the flicker of rowan
    And great curved ferns resolved themselves into a tune

That swayed about me and sung and trembled,
    And died as the long soft whirr of the wind had died
Leaving the dream-deep woodland shadow
    Lax as the tumbled down where the wild duck cried:

Till far off somewhere a rout of urchins
    Raised a clamour, nearer and yet more near,
That sank, and I saw them break toward the open,
    Under the branch-work, a moment, swift and clear,

Bearing each in his hands uprightly
    A green courageous clump of ferns that tossed
Their swooping fronds up on to the shoulders
    Of the running bearers as one by one they crossed,

Like an age-old sculpture suddenly living,
    A processional rite toward the very feet of the god.
Solemn and old and in triumph eternal,
    Earth offering earth, from earth, from the treader the trod.

And forever now on the wood's blurred margin,
  the frieze of pattering boys for me is hung,
Binding the sacrificial ages:
    Till the slow substantial wood where songs are sung

At idle whiles by the crisp or rainy
  Wind, and where glancing light and live things go,
Drifts like a ghostly dream about me,
    Unstable, insecure, a quivering show.

AUGUST 1919

PART IV

On Poets

The Poetry of Hugh MacDiarmid

To read Hugh MacDiarmid is a searing test of one's honesty. Can one be a believer and yet say, as the misbelieving men say, that he writes much pretentious nonsense? Love his work, yet confess his failures? The difficulty arises from the fanatical nature of the responses his work has evoked. Between "the only major poet writing in Europe to-day" and "the fellow's no poet - the merest charlatan" there seems no plain path for the feet. He has in fact a *daimon,* whether diabolic or divine, and to be sober in its presence is past praying for. One is under the influence at once, drunk with delight or furious in denunciation. Only the calm souls who don't know a *daimon* when they see it can read him calmly; and they, of course, have not read him at all.

I begin this study by stating that I am a believer: I believe he has qualities which are those of a major poet; I admit frankly to intoxication; I have been drunk for days together on a phrase, a cadence from his work. He can run plain words (*plain* words, the ordinary counters of our speech –not the half-made rock-hewn inventions of much modern poetry, including his own) into a sequence that is magical in its beauty, that "new-creates" the thing it says:

> Where he heard a port on the golden chanter
> That can never be heard by a fool —
>
> Cwa', een like milkwort and bog-cotton hair !
> I love you, earth, in this mood best o' a'—
>
> Cauld licht and tumblin' cloods —
>
> I never set een on a lad or a lass.

These are singing phrases, and MacDiarmid's greatness is in lyric: lyric, however, that is not mere emotion but passionate thought. His progress from the brief lyrics of *Sangschaw* and *Penny Wheep,* through the long soliloquy of *A Drunk Man Looks at the Thistle* and the gritty argumentative periods of *To Circumjack Cencrastus*, on to the immense bulk of the *Clann Albann* poem on which he is working in his Shetland retreat, need not obscure the issues. His lyric impulse changes, but the finest things in his work are still lyric in nature; only instead of singing phrases there are thoughts of the sort that reverberate deeper and deeper in one's consciousness as one dwells with them:

> It is necessary to go all the way at least
> And there are no fellow travellers.
>
> Everyman is the meaning and desire
> Of the world.

Gaily, daily, over abysses more ghastly
Men cast spider-webs of creation.

The inward gates of a bird are always open.
It does not know how to shut them.'

Sometimes these thoughts become almost gnomic and gnomic
verse might perhaps be regarded as lyric that is static rather
than flowing. The sound may not sing but the meaning does. It
is true that the sound sings progressively less in his later work, a
development that would seem to be intentional. In the *Lament
of the Great Music* he speaks of music that is

Deliberately cast in a non-rhythmic mould because the
composers knew
That rhythm is an animal function,

whereas poetry, as he sees it, in its highest manifestations
must be pure mind, freed from the wiles of the senses — "the
supreme reality is visible to the mind alone" — " hot blood is
of no use in dealing with eternity":

My love she is the hardest thocht
That ony brain can hae,
And there is nocht worth ha'en in life
That doesna lead her way.

Here, in the *Cencrastus* volume, the "hardest thoct" is still a
tune. This happens less often in the later volumes though the
lilt of Scots words on his tongue is nearly always tune. Their
rhythm, an "animal function," is in his blood.

This thought that is itself a passion, vital, dynamic, thrusting to the deepest sources of life, is the most important quality of his work. There are readers, however, who find themselves blocked before reaching it, whether by his absorption in politics, and therefore the propagandist, not to say polemical, character of some of his work; or his use of what has been called a private vocabulary, i.e. of words either newly coined, or drawn from sources so recondite, specialized and distant that the ordinary reader cannot hope to have met them. Both characteristics he shares with the other poets of his generation, and both are worth pause.

First, the matter of politics. The preoccupation of the younger poets of our day with politics is not only comprehensible but inevitable. The poet, like MacDiarmid's own skylark, may sing for himself alone:

> *You* cannot sing until your flight
> Leaves you no audience but the light —

yet no poet merely makes spontaneous sounds. Mind informs his music; and however startlingly original he may appear, he yet breathes in the mind of his age and cannot live without it. In a society that is sane, the poet, while transcending and transmuting the thought of his time, yet shares with it a tradition and an idiom. To call a poet great without this reciprocity is to speak without meaning: he cannot be recognized at all unless we share some mode of being with him.

He is a bold man who would claim for our present society that it is sane: or that it has a common tradition and idiom of spirit. The poet therefore is balked of this needful reciprocity, and he sets about restoring it by helping to create a condition of human society in which men will again hearken to poetry. He turns political. ("Literature ... cannot escape

triviality until it deals with events and issues that matter —
the death of an old order and the birth of a new." "It is not
in the ivory tower, but in active participation in the urgent
issues of the day, that a writer develops his gifts.") This is, of
course, nothing new. Shelley's "kingless continents sinless as
Eden," his "world's great age beings anew," were born out of
a political creed as urgent and specific as produced Spender's
Vienna.

MacDiarmid himself clearly recognizes this need for poetry
to be rooted in the common life:

> Are my poems spoken in the factories and fields,
>   In the streets o' the toon?
> Gin they're no, then I'm failin' to dae
>   What I ocht to hae dune.
>
> Gin I canna win through to the man in the street,
>   The wife by the hearth,
> A' the cleverness on earth'll no make up
>   For the damnable dearth.

He, too, asks of politics to provide a sane world. Yet he knows
that all policies are ephemeral —

> all the ideas
> That madden men now must lose their potency in a few years
> And be replaced by others —

and the essence of poetry is not touched by them. In a
consideration then, of his poetry, it might seem comfortable
to divide the man up, to say, There goes Grieve the politi-
cian, here MacDiarmid the poet. But that would be fatal, to
the poet. The man is one. Yet his particular political creed is

hardly relevant. What is relevant — with a fierce relevancy that focuses on everything he has written in a point of light — is the vision being his creed. That never changes. Always he sees man "filled with lightness and exaltation," living to the full reach of his potentialities. In that clear world, "all that has been born deserved birth." Man "will flash with the immortal fire," will

> rise
> To the full height of the imaginative act
> That wins to the reality in the fact,

until all life flames in the vision of

> the light that breaks
> From the whole earth seen as a star again
> In the general life of man.

The actuality is different. Men are obtuse, dull, complacent, vulgar. They love the third-rate, live on the cheapest terms with themselves, "the engagement twixt man and being forsaken," their "incredible variation nipped in the bud." Their reading is "novels and newspapers" their preoccupations, "fitba' and weemen." Iconoclasts and quacks "injure Creation," their thinking "treadmills of rationalizing,"

> The concoction instead of the experience,
> A sketchy intellectual landscape, not the search for the truth ...

> Out of the reach of perceptive understanding
> Forever taking place on the earth.

They have hardly yet issued

Up frae the slime, that a' but a handfu' o' men
Are grey wi' still.

They refuse to explores the largeness of life:

Consciousness spring frae unplumbed deeps.
 The maist o' men mak' haste
To kep odd draps in shallow thoughts
 And let the rest rin waste.
Quickly forgettin' ocht they catch
 Depends upon the kittle coorse
O' a wilder fount than they daur watch
Frae springin' in its native force
Against the darkness o' its source.

This refusal he sees as a cowardice. They

fear the cataract and like
Some spigot's drip instead,

and because of this fear

A' men's institutions and maist men's thocts
Are tryin' for aye to bring to an end
The insatiable thocht, the beautiful violent will,
The restless spirit of man.

If for the mass of men this picture is true, he believes that
human society must be wrongly ordered. Therefore the poet
demands a political change that will give men such living
conditions as may make the finer potentialities actual:

And have one glimpse of my beloved Scotland yet
As the land I have dreamt of where the supreme values
Which the people recognise are states of mind,
Their ruling passion the attainment of higher consciousness.

If then he sees the Douglas Credit System as an economic rule of life that will set men free from the shabby and niggardly anxieties of poverty, and Dialectical Materialism (issuing in Scots Republicanism) as the true nurturing ground of a culture that keeps individuality and distinction of mind and spirit, whether or not one agrees with these ideals, it is plain that they are accidental to this moment in history, and his vision of humanity's need remains valid beyond them. He is, therefore, more than the poet of a particular movement, and for his political opponents to condemn his poetry *because* they condemn his politics is like refusing a cup of cold water because one dislikes the colour of the cup.

Two charges must be met here: first, that much of his political verse is doggerel. I admit the charge. "The general public" is an incurably prosaic phrase, both in sound and in concept; nor will the most rabid of his admirers claim any value *as poetry* in

Come let us put an end to one thing
　Now that science gives us the power,
And make it impossible for any men
　To exercise for another hour
Any influence on other men that depends
　On economic pressure to gain its ends.

Second, that he is inconsistent. Admitted also: but the inconsistency has validity:

It is easy to cry
I am one with the working classes,
But no task in the world surpasses
In difficulty his who would try ...
Only by the severest intellectual discipline
Can one of the bourgeois intelligentsia win
Up to the level of the proletariat
On this side of the grave or that
— The only goal worth aiming at.
  O remorseless spirit that guides me
   The way seems infinite;
  What endless distance divides me
   From the people yet! ...

Let us climb to where the people can be found
  Ranged in their millions ...
This is the music of humanity—

this may seem to be cancelled out by

I am horrified by the triviality of life, by its corruption and
  helplessness,
All is soiled under philistine rule ...
Civilization has hitherto consisted in the diffusion and dilution
Of habits arising in privileged centres. It has not sprung from the
people.
It has arisen in their midst by a variation from them ...
A state composed exclusively of such workers and peasants
As make up most modern nations would be utterly barbarous.
Every liberal tradition would perish in it. The national and historic
Essence of patriotism itself would be lost, though the emotion no
  doubt
Would endure, for it is not generosity that the people lack.

They possess every impulse; it is experience they cannot gather,
For in gathering it they would be constituting the higher organs
That make up an aristocratic society—

or,

Great work cannot be combined with surrender to the crowd.

Yet even in the *Hymns to Lenin*, while he praises the vision and force of a great man's work, he sees clearly that an economic revolution is not enough:

> Your sphere's elementary and sune by
>   As a poet maun see't.
> Unremittin', relentless,
> Organized to the last degree,
> Ah, Lenin, politics is bairns' play
> To what this maun be !

It is therefore poetry, in its widest and deepest sense, that is the end to which all creation moves. Goethe is condemned as the poet "wha ootgrew Poetry." Faust turns to "drainage schemes, fashin' nae mair" with the supreme annunciation of the Word. This supreme annunciation springs from the deep common life of all mankind. The life-giving "word" may be spoken anywhere, the "new sang" that

> Alters the haill complexion o' life
> And maks a deid language o' a' we've kent

may come from anyone's lips.

For freedom means that a lad or a lass
 In Cupar or elsewhere yet
May alter the haill o' human thocht
 Mair than Christ's altered it.

I never set een on a lad or a lass
 But I wonder gin he or she
Wi' a word or deed'll suddenly dae
 An impossibility.

Yet

It's hard wark haud'n by a thocht worth ha'en
And harder speakin't, and no for ilka man.

The word of release, the "hardest thocht," implies an aristocracy, and the attitude of the world to the aristocrats of mind has been consistently inimical. They are denounced with Galileo, drink hemlock with Socrates, are crucified with Christ. If, therefore, MacDiarmid sees both that the poet must be cherished by the mass of the people as one with themselves, and yet hated and repudiated by them as one not of themselves, the dilemma is not his, but history's.

The matter of vocabulary. Poetry may be "private" as a result of unknown words, or of unknown associations. Both give to a poem an esoteric flavour. Here again we seem to meet a contradiction in one whose work is vowed to "the man in the street, the wife by the hearth." He invokes Rilke—

the marvellous obscurity of Rilke
Where what begin as metaphors all turn
To autonomous imaginative realities all pursuing
Their infinitely complicated ways.

Joyce—

> Wheesht, wheesht, Joyce, and let me hear
> Nae Anna Livvy's lilt,
> But Wauchope, Esk, and Ewes again,
> Each wi' its ain rhythms till't.

Doughty, whose craggy utterance, however (never half-hewn), is crystal compared with Joyce's and some of MacDiarmid's own.

Private words are a revolt against conventional emotion. If in using them the poet repudiates all those overtones and undertones of suggestion and association on which poetic effect depends (the allurement of "our little life is rounded with a sleep" against "our insignificant existence is terminated in a state of unconsciousness") — this is exactly his purpose, a gain and not a loss. For he sees words, as well as phrases, sicklied o'er, made sentimental through an excess of sentiment. "The dead in their nasty dead hands" have soiled them. Let's have new words therefore, to give our stark clean exact meaning, words not yet saturated with other people's meanings so that we have no guarantee at all that our readers will take our meaning from them. (Wordsworth, of course, was doing much the same thing over a century ago. It is the endless spiral of expression; and as slow time revolves, the past soaks out of the older words and we can use them again: even, if we have wit enough, for new meanings).

Words not charged with accustomed emotions are therefore needful to the pioneer. No one denies them to the scientist — why then to the adventurer in new modes of experience? This seems to me the position these word-hewers of our present-day poetry must be able to defend: that they have an experience of mind or spirit, a vision of truth, that cannot be expressed in current words without falsifying it. The over-charged word falsifies — but does the esoteric word communicate?

Here once more I admit (in my own case, and in such case one can only record one's own experience) much failure in communication. I stub my toe against boulders of words that make passage uneasy. Sometimes they yield a meaning to one's labour, sometimes not. But should the reading of poetry involve labour? Just here, I think, lies one of the intentions in these merciless words. One is made to realize that poetry is no slick affair, one is braced to meet its demands. The result is a keen exhilaration and expectancy. But expectancy is not an end in itself. Roused awareness is a primary need for all poetic experience, but the final resolution must be to a deep and sure content. In a brief poem, *In the Foggy Twilight,* MacDiarmid himself suggests how hard it is to achieve this rounding of the substance of one's experience into form. He watches

> Moisture getherin' slowly on the heather cowes
> In drops no' quite heavy eneuch to fa'.
>
> And I kent I was still like that
> Wi' the spirit o' God, alas!
> Lyin' in wait in vain for a single grey drop
> To quicken into perfect quidditas.

When the achieved form teases the reader, the final miracle of acceptance cannot be wrought. So while strange words sharpen our mood and quicken thought, they must be lived with before they can give us full poetic satisfaction. (This "living" process is not a matter of time so much as of power of entry.) I feel then that experimentation like MacDiarmid's is healthy, and will ultimately enlarge the borders of expression (and what poet has not felt them too narrow?) though what will survive and be part of the future does not depend on him, but on others' dealings with what he has given them.

In this strange philologist's underworld, I personally have found most delight from the long opening paragraph of *On a Raised Beach,* where the poet is evoking one of those moments of recognition in which we see something familiar as though for the first time and know it with a sort of primordial knowledge. Stones : to have seen them as he sees them here is an astonishment. His sense of their utter strangeness, their *stone-ness,* their sharp hard identity, demands words that will rake aside all stock description.

In *Water Music* and *Scots Unbound* he is attempting the same effect for the movement and colour of water (this water poem is one of his most musical), for the colours, scents and textures of the world. And to senses that are keen and aware, words will always fail to catch the multitudinous differences that make the possession of the five senses such a joy. Yet for all his uncanny and subtle skill in expression these infinite distinctions, I feel that I would give his whole phalanx of words for one of his swift illuminating metaphors.

For, putting aside philosophy and philology, what matters in poetry is neither meaning nor vocabulary, but the fusion of both in utterance that is itself an experience. Such utterance MacDiarmid has, in single words, both in English ("and in the stone *Obliviously* sleeps a strength Beyond our own") and in Scots ("a sudden lowe o' fun," "the gurly thistle," "scrunts o' blooms," "gealed an' rankled auld bluid-vessels" "pig slorpin' owre't") in phrases and in imagery. His metaphors, like Rilke's, become "autonomous imaginative realities." He is, in fact, a *makar,* creating new life.

The profound mystery of creation itself, brooded over, eternally beyond explanation, moves him profoundly:

> Now I deal with the hills at their roots

And the streams at their springs
And am to the land that I love
　　As he who brings
His bride home, and they know each other
Not as erst, like their friends, they have done,
But carnally, causally, knowing that only
By life nigh undone can life be begun,
　　And accept and are one.

Yet

Licht thraws nae licht upon itself.

Mystery must remain the heart of creation:

For closer than gudeman can come
And close to'r than hersel',
What didna' need her maidenheid
Has wrocht his purpose fell.

O wha's been here afore me, lass,
And hoo did he get in?
　　　—A man that deed or I was born
　　　This evil thing has din.

And left, as it were on a corpse,
Your maidenheid to me?
　　　—Nae lass, gudeman, sin Time began
　　　's hed ony mair to gi'e

　　　But I can gi'e ye kindness, lad,
　　　And a pair o' willin' hands,

And you sall hae my breists like stars,
My limbs like willow wands,

And on my lips ye'll heed nae mair,
And in my hair forget,
The seed o' all the men that in
My virgin womb has met ...

There is indeed in this man, in some quarters regarded as a mere unmannerly tub-thumper, a mystic apprehension so sensitive and aware that there is no mode of expression for it but metaphor — "the mad leap into the symbol." The lovely *Herd of Does* illustrates this sensitive delicacy:

> There is no doe in all the herd
>   Whose heart is not her heart,
> O Earth, with all their glimmering eyes
>   She sees thee as thou art.
>
> Like them in shapes of fleeting fire
>   She mingles with the light
> Till whoso saw her sees her not
>   And doubts his former sight.
>
> They come and go and none can say
>   Who sees them subtly run
> If they indeed are forms of life
>   Or figments of the sun . . .
>
> But now and then a wandering man
>   May glimpse as on he goes
> A golden movement of her dreams
>   As 'twere a herd of does.

Other metaphors are condensed to a startling clarity. Earth, in company of the shining planets, is a "bonnie broukit bairn", earth's earthiness, its lovableness, succinctly expressed.

> I'm fu' o' a stickit God,
> That's what's the maitter wi' me,

embodies unforgettably the conception of an evolving God, struggling through man towards his own development. Life itself is the coiled snake, uncoiling with the process of history, its moments of beauty "a glisk o' the serpent walloping":

> Flashing, wise, sinuous, dangerous creature,
> Offspring of mystery and the world without end—

though to the spiritually dead the snake is only a "property snake." The "important people," snug with labels, complacent holders of certificates, crowding the good positions, are "performing fleas"

> Guid sakes, ye dinna need to pass
> Ony exam to dee
> —Daith canna tell a common flech
> Frae a performin' flea !

In Eternity, "swack souls are nae mair clogged wi' clay." From the tomb in Moscow flashes "the eternal lightning of Lenin's bones." The vision of angels — "they bleezin' trashy French-like folk" — fixes for ever the mental delimitations of Crowdieknowe. The poet prays he may never be

> Like standin' water in a pocket o'
> Impervious clay.

He wearies "tyauvin' wi' this root-hewn Scottis soul." His "mind hawk-steadies owre the moore," his life is built on shifting sand, and he can

> Feel the filthy grit gang grindin'
> Into my brain's maist delicate windin'.

He has moments of vision that penetrate like X-rays—the living will be "stricken ghastly in eternal light."

But the external world of actuality is to be seen not only in the mirror of image. He can describe it directly, with graphic incisiveness. The thistle is "a' shank and jags," the hillsides "lirk like elephant skins" as one passes through a tumble of their brown shapes. At the Cattle Show he sees

> Stylish sheep, with fine heads and well-woolled,
> And great bulls mellow to the touch,
> Brood mares of marvellous approach, and geldings
> With sharp and flinty bones and silken hair.

The oceans of the north and the south are contrasted:

> Not in a swift ship over the blue Aegean sea,
> Or fishing boat leaping to the flash
> Of red oars in the early sunlight
> In Phaleron Bay, but over cold knotted hacking waters.

Age comes on, and

> The elbuck fankles in the coorse o' time,
> The sheckle's no' sae souple, and the thrapple
> Grows deef and dour: nae langer up and doun
> Gleg as a squirrel speils the Adam's apple.

Persons start up from the pages, complete in a phrase, their whole environment implied. Such is the mother fo the *fleggit bride,* implacably experienced:

> Seil o' yer face! the send has come.
> I ken, I ken, but awa' ye gan,
> An dinna fash, for what's in her hert
> A' weemun ken an' nae man can.
>
> Seil o' yer face! Ye needna seek
> For comfort gin ye show yer plight.
> To Gods an' men, coorse callants baith,
> A fleggit bride's the silfu' sicht.

Such are the

> Muckle men wi' tousled beards
> I grat at as a bairn,

and Focherty, high-coloured, hard-drinking, who stumps through others' lives "like a muckle rootless tree":

> Blae-faced afore the throne o' God
> He'll get his fairin' yet.

His pictures can be disconcerting in the extreme. When he attacks complacency, humbug, the second-rate, he flicks on the raw. A fleering laughter pursues the quarry. To certain divins he is as merciless as was Burns:

> Try on your wings ; I ken vera weel
> It wadna look seemly if ony ane saw
> A Glasgow Divine ga'en flutherin' aboot

In his study like a drunk craw.

But it' ud look waur if you'd to bide
   In an awkward squad for a month or mair
Learnin' to flee afore you could join
   Heaven's air gymnkhana aince you get there.

The politician appears in an equally undignified posture, when the Lion Rampant ceases to be a mere dead symbol and comes alarmingly avile:

   O the lion is aff the flag again
   And reengin' the countryside,

with the politician of our poet's abhorrence in its mouth, "lum hat and spats a' complete":

   O the lion is oot o' the flag again
      And whasae leases a moor
   'll aiblins get mair than he bargains for
      Gin he disna ken the spoor.

The sheer gusto of this vigorous vision is a delight. Few livelier things have been written in our generation. Thank God for a lion in

   a country whaur turnin' a corner
   You could lippen on nocht but a sheep !

Ramping through the land the Lion meets first one of the enemies of his country's good ("and crunched him for a stert"), then another, and another ("and bashed them wi' a paw").

The same derisive scorn is poured on the poet "wha ootgrew poetry"

> And Goethe never wat his feet
>   But had the water laid on —
> Baith H. and C. nor kent nor cared
>   The deeps his pipes made raid on …
>   But Oh! that the Heavens had opened and let
>   A second Flood on this plumbers' pet !

Superb gusto is also in the Drunk Man, *stoiterin' hame* by moonlight, in whose path rises a gaunt shaggy shape — The Thistle. Thistle and Man confront each other, a life for a life. The Man is *raised* — at that glorious stage of drink when life has no riddle left to solve. He glowers at the Thistle, reading truth after truth from its thrawn humours, till he can hardly tell if what he sees *is* thistle,

> Or my ain skeleton through wha's bare banes
> A fiendish wund's begood to whistle.

He may indeed be only dreaming this jaggy shape:

> For a' I ken I'm safe in my ain bed.
> *Jean! Jean!* Gin *she's* no' here it's no oor bed,
> Or else I'm dreamin' deep and canna wauken,
> But it's a fell queer dream if this is no'
> A real hillside — and thae things thistles and bracken !

Perhaps *he* is the dream, or else a thing

> Preserved in spirits in a muckle bottle, …
> Mounted on a hillside, wi' the thistles
> And bracken for verisimilitude.

Slowly it is driven in on him that he and this chance-met obstacle to his passage home, which he addresses there in his drunken fervour, have changed identities; that here in the Thistle he can contemplate himself, a "dumbfoondrin' growth," the strain of matter "twined in sic an extraordinary way"

> that gied it sic a guise
> As maun hae pleased its Makar wit' a gey surprise.

Yet to root the Thistle from his nature (or from the Scots nature) is to leave

> nocht but naethingness there,
> The hole whaur the Thistle stood.

Nothing remains but to be oneself – the final honesty, and the hardest but for all the "datchie jags," the "reishlin' stalk" and "gausty leafs,"

> gleids o' central fire
> In its reid heids escape.

The Thistle, from

> Blin' root to bleezin' rose
> Through a' the whirligig
> O' shanks and leafs and jags

is a "bramble yokin' earth and heaven,"

> Roses to lure the lift
> And roots to wile the clay,

and the Thistle, like every other form of life, has its own perfection:

> The munelicht that owre clear defines
> The thistle's shrill cantankerous lines
> E'en noo while's insubstantialises
> Its grisly form and 'stead devises
> A maze o' licht, a siller-frame,
> As 'twere God's dream frae which it came,
> Ne'er into bein' coorsened yet,
> The essence lowin' pure in it.

With the bewildering speed with which he changes his metaphors, a few pages further on the Wheel of Life spins,

> And on a birlin' edge I see
> Wee Scotland squattin' like a flea,
> And dizzy with the speed, and me!

These bewildering changes of mood and metaphor, of image and intention are inescapable in his work. They are part of the amazing fecundity of the man. 'Gleids o' central fire' escape in a thousand forms. Men do well to fear him, since fire is formidable, and even those who scoff, "glowering" callously, may

> Yet slow but surely heat until
> You catch my flame against your will
> And the mureburn taks the hill.

Marion Angus

Marion Angus was not wholly human. A sprite was in her. Her elfin quality was obvious to anyone who read her poetry; but she was impish as well as elfin — a Puck. Whiles, one would think, she was inhabited by the very Mischief.

This was a side of her that found little expression in her poetry — there is a pale reflection of it in "Wee Jock Todd." She was capable, even at the age of 80, of playing small, solemn, practical jokes, schoolboy jokes, but much more intelligent. Her jokes had point — they pricked. They pricked where she wanted them to prick — in the quick of dullness and pretentiousness and stupidity. She could do disconcerting things, like tearing a few pages from a book to indicate that it was poor stuff, or deliberately understamping a letter to a pompous dame who was niggardly with her pence.

Her speech, too, had the devastating candour of a four-year-old's. Told that a certain gentleman was bewildered by one of her poems, she answered tartly: 'He would be.' As she grew deafer, she would describe, in company, in a loud voice, the shortcomings of someone who was present. Her listeners were embarrassed, but excused her on the grounds of her deafness;

she could not know how loud she was talking. I have a shrewd suspicion that she knew very well how loud she was talking. Her asides were stage asides, meant to penetrate the corners.

Once I was summoned urgently to see her. An unknown man had written, asking for a copy of an early poem of hers, not reprinted, as the best of them were, in a later volume, and for permission to use it in an anthology. She had no copies of her own works, she didn't even remember how it went, but she was sure that it was poor, and she disliked being represented by it. Had I the early book? I had. I found the poem, agreed with her estimate of it, typed it out for her, and, not having time to write a covering letter, wrote in faint pencil beneath the text an acid comment on the taste of the man who chose it. When I next saw her, she told me with a wicked glint that she had sent him the poem, comment and all. I remonstrated. She said: 'It will do him good.'

Marion Angus was a wilding slip from her solid stock, though their more sober virtues were in her, too. She had their rectitude, unfeigned piety and courtesy. Of her father, a minister in Arbroath, it was said that "he treated the mill-girls as if they were Duchesses". She, too, had a charm of courtesy towards the unimportant, and a deference that had not the smallest trace of servility towards those whom she considered great. When you went to see her, the welcome she gave you miraculously enlarged your own personality. To young writers, often quite unknown to her, she would give patient help and criticism. There must be many a manuscript extant that has been seen by only her eyes and the eyes of its maker. And the generosity of her judgments, in one whose tongue could be so caustic, was fabulous. At one time, W.H. Auden, then a young schoolmaster, used to drop in to read her his verses. He, of course, was seeking not advice, but what we in the North-East call "addisens"; and as an audience she was perfect. If she sighed a little because the subsequent discussion was all about him and never about her, she never, one imagines, made him aware of it. She was, I am afraid, a most accomplished flatterer; she could be enchantingly benign, and she could be a gypsy.

The gypsy strain in her, a dole, perhaps from some 'lang-deid wumman o' ma kin' came out in many ways. It came out in the flaunting scarlet scarves she loved to wear in her younger days, in the flamboyant covers of her earlier Porpoise Press volumes, in her recklessness of speech, her passion for the splendour of life,

> . ... *red-legged partridges*
> *And the golden fishes of the Duc de Guise,*

above all, in her untamed heart. In old age, she did not sit back, serene, with passion spent and desire quieted in her. She was not serene. She still desired. She never quite forgave the disabilities of her failing flesh. I have never known anyone so hungry for vicarious experience. She wanted to know all that one did, and saw, all the people one met, the odd things one encountered. There was greed in her eyes as she asked, glee as she listened, and a sort of envy in her voice as she said, of things that were often humdrum enough: "What an interesting life you have."

Interesting — that was the dynamic word. She couldn't bear to be dull. To have a life and not use it, not savour it to the full — that moved her to contempt. To have the capacity to savour, but not the opportunity — that was her private torment. She had never had enough of the glory and the colour of living. Her life had held no excitement but the excitement of poetry; and she was an incurable romantic in that she always expected life to be more splendid than it is in the nature of life to be. Like any green girl, she wanted things to happen; and, to the last, that obstinate and wilful life in her would not be stilled.

This, I think, is why so many people have found that her poetry springs from frustration. Unhappy love — love betrayed, love unrequited, love sated —

> *Love is fine, fine,*
> *But it doesna bide—*

is dominant in her verses. And she herself tells us quite clearly in "Waater o' Dye" that she has "niver kent … the luve o'men."

> *Waater o'Dye, whaur ye rin still*
> *On me she warks her auncient will;*
> *What I hae niver kent, I ken—*
> *The feel o' babes, the luve o' men.*

Yet in the face of this naked confession one had best be wary; she knows a very great deal about human nature in love. She claims that her knowledge came through her 'possession' by a dead woman. I should call it rather imaginative apprehension.

She understands the despairing self-disgust of a smirched woman to whom a second chance has come.

> *Singin' waater, rin oot o' the sna',*
> *Syne doon by the breckan green ;*
> *Oh, wad ye bit tak' ma grief awa'*
> *An' mak' ma hert clean.*

She understands the cruelty in an unattractive woman, who watches her lover drawn away from her.

> *My skin is broon as a toad,*

111

E'en hae I shairp's a shrew,
Ma hert is black an' coorse,
  Coorse thro' an, 'thro.
For better ye wad hae fared,
  Ma bonnie young barefit quean,
Hedna the lad I lo'e
  Cum whistlin' ower the green.

She knows that to have wronged is a sharper agony than to be wronged.

But whaur, o' skilly spae-wife,
Whaur is growin' green,
The sweet leaf o' healin'
Will soothe my sleepless een
And gar me greet nae langer
The hurt that I hev' gi'en?

She knows the timelessness of a possession that is of the spirit, though the lovers may meet "wi, mortal fit — nae mair." She knows the terror of the girl compelled through the revelations of a "fortune wife" to face the fear she has not hitherto allowed to rise into consciousness.

Siller eneuch hid I tae spare
For a wee blue boat frae the Mairket Fair …

I bocht a brooch wi' a siller pin,
A kerchief for tyin' anaith ma chin ;
A' the lave o' the money went
Tae the fortune wife in the gipsy tent.

The Corbie Burn's ayont the Dee—

> *Wi' cauld white lips it girned at me;*
> *The witch frae oot o' the ha'thorn luikt,*
> *Wi' a' her ten black fingers crookt.*

> *The fowk that bides in the Deid Man's Cairn*
> *They chittered, chittered amang the fern:*
> *"Here cams the maid that hadna a groat*
> *Tae buy a wee laddie a wee blue boat.*

She knows the cold relief when a passion is dead—

> *Sin' noo we twa maun twine*
> *Wi' nae mair troth tae keep*
> *My hert wins oot o' the kist*
> *Whaur ye lockit it doon sae deep—*

and the reluctance of a girl to be emotionally involved by a passion which she cannot share. When the young man "pits his hert-brek in a sang" and the sang runs "ower a' the braes o'Dee," then she is involved for as long as the song is remembered, and against her will. "O I hae gien wha wadna gie." I have heard this exquisite line interpreted as a seduction; what the interpreter makes of the rest of the poem I can't think. The innocence of the boy's love is clearly seen in the delicate presents he brings the girl:

> *He brocht me troots frae lochans clear,*
> *A skep o' bees, a skin o' deer.*

One is in the very morning of the world.

If, therefore, her themes are few and her range narrow, her experience is not narrow. It is sure and true. She has the power — and what is that but creation? — to experience the things that did not happen to her. There is here a consummation of a very rare order.

An interesting light is shed on her narrowness of range by her own choice among the great things in Scots poetry. Some years ago at the end of a term spent on Scots literature, I asked a class of students to make their own choice of the twelve greatest Scottish poems. Then, as kitchie to their effort, I made the same request to half a dozen well-known outsiders. Whereas a poet like William Soutar, who also played in the game, put "The Golden Targe," "The Testament of Cresseid," and "Tam o' Shanter," on his list, Marion Angus chose exclusively lyrics, and lyrics where the haunted and the yearning note predominates: "The Flowers o' the Forest," "Aye Waukin' O," "Proud Maisie," "Waly, Waly," "Gone were but the Winter Cold," "O Wert Thou in the Cauld Blast". Now anyone who has discussed books with her knows how wide and varied her reading was, how quick her mind and catholic her appreciation; but it would seem that for her the heart of the mystery lay in pure lyric.

I have emphasised the solidity of her knowledge of men and women because so much has been made of the glimmer that lies upon her work. Yet, even though lyric was the element of her spirit, she knew very well that man does not live by honey-dew alone. She may take us to the edge of discoverable experience —

> *I heard my name at gloamin' late,*
> *I heard it cried sae clear and sma',*
> *But ere my fit was at the yett*
> *The wind had blawn the soond awa'*—

but she is also native to its heart. The folk on whom her delicate perception is exercised are the plain folk of a Scottish countryside. She sees them with relish —

> *I aye likit my Grannie's sister,*
> *Her, that carried the fisher creel.*
> *She sang a wee thing rauch and timmer*
> *Nor kent nae lilt nor reel.*
> *She cam' from the cauld east countra,*
> *I likit her rael weel—*

with an astringent humour, as in the widow who regrets that her husband would not have "respeckit" on his tombstone; with tenderness, as in the auld wife asking the bairns for news of the old cobbler, whom nobody likes,

> *Grim wi' sorrow*
> *An' grey wi' greed …*
> *He was my ain luve*
> *In the green glen-heid.*

She is particularly good with old women—

> *Juist a dune wife*
> *Greetin' in her plaid—*

or the old woman who remembers her own fear of meeting a witch when a child says to her:

> *"Ye'r sma-bookit,*
> *Yer broo's runkled sair,*
> *Er' ye the auld witch*
> *O' the Briad Hill o' Fare?"*

These folk have their feet firmly set on the soil of the North-East.

I kent him by his heather step
An' the turn upon his tongue.

The landscape is nor'-eastern, and so is the weather; like all Scots poets, she evokes the sinister better than the gentle airs.

An' curse the wind for an auld grey foumart.

Or,

She hard the leaf reistlin'
Cauld amang snaw,
Ae bird cheepin'
'Tween a water an' a wa'.

The north names make singing tunes in her verse — Culblean and Cambus; Tarland and Inverey; the Water o' Dye and the Corby Burn and the Braid Hill o' Fare. She had a strong feeling for the potency in names. Once when I had sent her a root of rosemary, she wrote: "I have planted the rosemary in the garden here and pronounced your name three times over it." An incantation lightly spoken; but incantation, one feels, was real to her. Her poetry, indeed, is incantation. It sings, and its singing is its purpose. Its lovely cadences are integral to its meaning. As with most Scottish poets, her cadences run most liltingly in Scots, but she can make even English sing:

Complaining to each other
With lamentable lips
For the great dead captains
And the old sailing ships.

But the things that sing themselves into the mind and stay there are Scots:

I wad hae gi'en him my lips tae kiss
Had I been his, had I been his;
Barley breid and elder wine,
Had I been his as he is mine.

One may find an occasional echo of Housman and of Rossetti, but for the most part her note was quite her own, as individual to her as its scent is to the wild thyme. It is as a fragrance that she lingers in the memory, a fragrance with a tang to it, grateful and fresh.

Charles Murray

Charles Murray was a man one could not miss in a company. He had presence: not self-assertive, but dynamic — one felt more alive from being with him. When he spoke, he had compulsive listeners. Droll, witty, solemn, seemingly nonchalant but with a delighted relish in what he related, he was a raconteur of genius. He was company for Duke or ditcher, and imperturbably himself with both. His lean hawk face was warm with interest — sheer simple interest in people, what they were, what they did, how they did it. He noticed things: which is why the detail in his poems is so lively and so right. The perennial freshness of his interest in folk, not only for their sterling qualities but for their quirks and inadequacies, absurdities and sins, was basic to his character and to his verse.

Why they did what they did was not his concern. There is nothing introspective, no psychological probing; his poetry is a poetry of externals, yet at its best his selection of externals is so vital that his portrayal not only portrays but illuminates. Towards intellectual and symbolic poetry he was wary, not convinced of its validity, but willing to concede it its right to be — humble towards it as he was in much else. He did not for instance reveal his identity to the master mason (when he himself was Secretary for Public Works to the Government of the Union of South Africa and the new Government buildings were going up in Pretoria, he being responsible for the enterprise) who asked, eyeing the rather rough-looking man who had sat down on a stone and newsed with him in his own North-East dialect, 'Was ye wantin' a job?' — 'I've gotten a job.' — 'Ye're lucky.' The mason of course discovered later who he was and was to say, 'It was me that speired if ye was wantin' a job.' An encounter that went straight to Charles Murray's heart.

It is unfortunate that his reputation outside the North-East, for nostalgic and rather facile verse, has congealed on the early editions of *Hamewith* and the anthology pieces, which do not contain his mature work. Later work was stronger and more powerfully knit. He became a master of compression. Thus a quite ordinary concept like supperless to bed condenses into *beddit boss*. In the eight lines of *Noo that cauldrife winter's here* a whole way of life, at a given time and place, in a given society, is crystallised. Five statements and the thing is done. One brief line alone, *Butter skites an' wunna spread,* reverberates in the mind, calling up one picture after another of what it meant to live in the country, in Scotland, in bitter weather, in the late nineteenth and early twentieth century. He does not need to elaborate, the reader's mind flies out to meet his own. The goodness of this tiny poem lies partly in its power to evoke and partly in the perfection of its form, but largely also in the subtle way two experiences of life play upon each other, of those to whom these hardships are hard, and of the reminiscent man who sees them across many African summers and recalls them with an affectionate chuckle. This is a device by which he conveys many of his effects. Straight-faced he can say

> *Naked tho' we're born an' equal*
> *Lucky anes are made police,*

but out of the corner of our eye we catch the glint in his.

He is especially good on winter, as what Scottish poet is not? The Southron may claim that our grim climate turns us into frozen and inanimate clods, but we know that instead it releases our perceptiveness. So Murray is following in the tracks of Gavin Douglas and Henryson and Burns when he writes *mochie or makin' for snaw* and we can feel the two different kinds of chill. *Drift oxter-deep haps Bennachie* — this cunning line cannot be spoken aloud without effort, as though we were floundering ourselves in the drift. He excels in making the movement of a line reflect its feeling. *Up Bennachie I'm rivin' on* gives the very feel of the hill-climber pressing on to his goal. Contrast its soaring inflection with the heavy tread of the mourners at a country funeral — *An face in fun'ral blacks the drift aince mair* — or the eager lightness of the flocks in spring —

> *The sheep are aff to the hills again*
> *As hard as the lambs are able*

Lines like these show how meticulous he was as an artist. Poems that seem to bubble up like a natural spring are often wrought with extreme care and much revision; he was not satisfied till he had words and movement right.

It is a narrow world that he deals with, the Vale of Alford set among its surrounding hills (and what a roll-call he gives of our Northern hills—

> *There's Tap o' Noth, the Buck, Ben Newe,*
> *Lonach, Ben Rinnes, Lochnagar ...*

> *But Bennachie! Faith yon's the hill*
> *Rugs at the hairt when ye're awa'!*

but narrow though it is, it is realised with an intense clarity: its winds and weathers, its *caul' coorse simmer only gweed for girse,* its *snaw-bree in the Leochel Burn,* its *burstin' buds on the larick,* its foalies and teuchats, *its fite-fuskered cat wi' her tail i' the air,* its *craps weel in an' stackit.* But, with that abiding interest in people that marked him first and last, it is his lovable array of human beings that provokes his finest work — his ill-trickit loons, his kitchen-deemies, his country craftsmen. *The Packman* is a shrewd study, not very profound, the miller, in the poem of that name, dust in his throat, is wise —

> *Afore they can judge o' my drinkin'*
> *They first maun consider my drooth*

Most delicately rendered is Jeames, whose misdemeanours, of which his wife Nell keeps him in constant remembrance, are counterbalanced by *the mony patient years he bore wi' Bell,* who for all her disapproval, survived him only a fortnight. The real tenderness with which Jeames and Bell are portrayed is not destroyed but enhanced by the ribald description of Bell's translation to Heaven —

> *Just when he thocht to slip awa' at last ...*
> *The muckle gates aboon were barely fast*
> *Ere she was pechin' up the gowden stair ...*

The same literal-mindedness over heaven — the speaker serious, the poet amused — is seen in an affectionate late pendant to the early *Jeames, Yokin' the Mear,* where husband and wife disagree over the after-life; *she hankers for heaven, I'm canty doon here ... The wife can hae feathers but I'm for a gig.* Even God Himself *daunders furth to some clood edge* to look at the earth mankind has connached.

This conception of the godhead, bodied in the tough Aberdeenshire speech, is his people's as much as the poet's. Murray's Scots is always the Aberdeenshire tongue, as spoken in the Vale of Alford in his youth. He carried it in the ear, not the eye through books, and so he can render the run of the voice, the spoken intonation. There is a speaker implicit in every poem, in *There's aye a something* as much as in *Dokens afore his peers.* This is why he is right, for his purposes, in using the local idiom — why he takes his Aberdeenshire Scots neat.

Of those where the speaker is also the dominant figure, two poems of the First World War come nearest of all to greatness. In *Dockens afore his peers* and *Fae France* a society is seen in depth because its rural affairs are acted out against a larger and grimmer background. Both poems are written in the first person, so that both speakers are self-revealed but reveal at the same time, in the most natural manner imaginable, as something that needed no explanation but just was, a whole complex of relationships that are put to the test against the experience of war. The portrait of Dockens is a magnificent crag of a thing. Self-opinionated, garrulous, utterly insensitive, completely blind to all that lies outside the range of his immediate interest, sure of his power, without scruple or manners but with a tremendous vitality, he attends an exemption tribunal with one purpose only in his mind, to win exemption for his youngest son: and wins it. From his entry, *O ay, I'll sit, birze ben a bit,* we have a measure of the man. There follows his (uncalled-for) diatribe against the war:

> *A' the fash we've had wi' fowk gyaun aff afore the term ...*
> *We've nane to spare for sojerin', that's nae oor wark ava.*

Interrupted, he gives a list of the folk on his farm, a graphic and lively list. Of all the kitchen-deems that Charles Murray has portrayed, the deem at Dockenhill is the non-pareil, good-hearted, willing, but rude as you make them — *big an' brosy, reid an' roch an' swippert as she's stoot.* But when he reaches his youngest, and sees that all his ingenuity is not to get the laddie off, he rounds on the Tribunal and in a whirlwind of primal force lays bare his power:

Hoot, Mains, hae mind, I'm doon for you some sma' thing wi' the bank;
Aul' Larickleys, I saw you throu', an' this is a' my thank;
An' Gutteryloan, that time ye broke, to Dockenhill ye cam' ...

It is enough. Exemption is awarded.

"Total exemption." Thank ye, sirs. Fat say ye till a dram?

The last line is brilliant. Without a word of comment, out of his own mouth the poet has exposed the man for what he is, so coarse and insensitive that he expects men to drink with him who he has thus publicly scarified. This is portrait-painting in masterly vein. There is also of course, a side *sklint* at the me who abrogate their public duty to save their own face.

Fae France is in the form of a letter, the writer a farm servant who for breach of the peace has been fined by the Shirra. It *took a sax month's fee* to cover fine and lawyer and drinks, and he was able to meet it only by a little judicious poaching. As he later joins up in the local regiment and his officer is the Shirra's son, a young man who can talk to him in his own dialect, has certainly been a country boy, and knows all about his randy past including the poaching, one can hardly be mistaken in supposing the Shirra to be a local laird — it may even have been from his own preserves that the fine was paid. At the front the young officer is thoroughly approved by his men because he knows their idiom and when he asks for volunteers for a night raid, the poacher is up and off; and is the one, when the officer is wounded, to hoist him on his back and save his life. Later the boy's mother writes to thank him. Between the lines one can sense the poacher's pride in the letter, though in true north-country style he will not give himself away and covers his own emotion by a nice touch of deprecation.

> *His mither sent a letter till's, a great lang blottit screed.*
> *It wasna easy makin't ott, her vreetin's coorse to read.*

And in true north-country style, when asked by the mother what she can give him to show her gratitude, he will not be rewarded —

> *Jist bid yer man, fan neist I'm up, ca' canny wi' the fine.*

The interaction of these persons, country land-owner who is also sherriff, son who is officer in what was then a local regiment, farm servant who fights both in and out of the army, with their tangle of loyalties accentuated by the war, lights up an authentic part of our social history.

As indeed does all his verse. It is a record of a way of living already altered and of customs and conventions that have vanished. But it is more than a record, it is an affirmation, of life. These poems have the glow of health on them. Their verve and gusto are the outward and visible sign of an inward assurance that life is livable and mankind worth knowing. The seed of Charles Murray's power is that he said yes to life.

PART V

Prose Pieces

Smuts

There are sublunary smuts and smuts, like Caesar's wife, above all suspicion — you would never dream of them. These glittering spangly specks, these wandering fires, these beads in the celestial kaleidoscope, these gaudy flies that dance in eternal revolution through mazes eternally renewed - in short (in a burst of confidence) the stars: what are they but Brobdingnagian smuts in the cold unsullied immaculate monotony of space? Tut! 'tis a wicked generalisation, that things above ground can be profitably likened to things above space, to the better understanding of the latter. Rather is it the things of the imagination that enlighten us regarding the things of the senses. Stars explain smuts, not smuts stars. That same cold immaculate monotony would freeze us with horror were it not for the kindly confetti of its stars. Smuts have the same comfortable *bonhomie*. Perfection and vice are equally repellent, but smuts, perforce postulating perfection, yet relieve it. They temper it to the little human sheep. We take our perfection, like our oaths, diluted. Administer it neat, and we kick.

Mankind has therefore an inborn predilection for these evanescent creatures of a moment. Accuse him therefore and he will deny it. But in childhood, before "ars est celare" and such-like snippets become the bugbear and bogy of a social existence, he reveals his true appreciations with ingenuous delight. Away with the "priest-like" task of pure ablution round earth's human shores'! In childhood at least the healthy human instinct refuses to be priest-ridden. Deliver us, good deity, from the peril by water! ...

Yet I maintain, and shall do till I die, that the child is incapable of a true appreciation of the smut. The full-bellied substantiality of mud is rather his idol. He makes of his god a savoury mess that he may eat thereof — a mud pie. The smut — save when it alights on someone else's nose — is of too fine, too rarefied an essence for his young capacities. Its very elusiveness, the guarantee of its perennial fascination, is fatal to its popularity — 'tis caviare to the general. Yet the sure delicacy of its good-breeding deserves a better fate. Consider Dr. Slop, bespattered, beluted, transubstantiated by the unmannerly Shandy mud; Parson Adams, slobbered over by the immortal slime of Mr Trulliber's pig-sty—your smut, now, would never have insulted these worthies so. Mischievous it may be, upon occasion naughty, but it is at least polite. It knows its place — though you do not. You transfix it, and it is gone. An Ariel, black but comely; a snowflake has not more grace nor languor; a feather by comparison is gross. But — there is always a *Cave*, else what a house of cards might we not build on this frail foundation of the smut — trust it not; it will not stand forever betwixt you and the Absolute; 'tis not in grain, sir; it will wash off.

Pixies and Or'nary Peoples

The formula does not vary. Every night when I look round the door her finger beckons, an arm steals to my neck and pulls my head to the pillow, and she whispers, so low that I could hardly tell the words were it not that I know them already: "Is there a story about a pixie?" That over, she lies smiling at me with a smile that is almost maternal in its tender delighted possessiveness. "Any or'nary peoples now?" she says.

The classification is her own; and though she is able now on any common occasion to say *ordinary people* in the common way, for this purpose the phrase retains its dew. It is no longer a phrase. It is a name. It signifies one of the two great divisions of the Kingdom of Story.

And I am persuaded that her classification is valid. If I substitute terms of my own for hers — the sea-coast of Bohemia and Main Street, Prometheus and Soames Forsyte — I touch the two allurements that from time immemorial have wiled men to the story-teller. They listen because he tells them what they know already: or because he tells them what may not be known. Both are necessary — both mystery and certitude. I love a broom-stick, and also a walking stick. I want the moon and the Pleiades and buttons to fasten my coat. I have followed "in the forests of the night" the chase of the Burning Tiger, but

I have also an important affection for my hen High-stepper. Out of these things, buttons and broom-sticks, moonshine and a mother hen, literature has been made, and it would be hard to tell which is the more beloved — whether the "pale kings and princes too, pale warriors" or "Jerusalem, Jerusalem, how often would I have gathered thy children" whether Othello's "I have a sword of Spain, the ice-brook's temper" or Lear's "Pray you, undo this button." Are the supreme moments of human experience very strange or very simple, the best tales wild or plain. I think, both. We classify, but there is no real dividing line. Fire is in every habitation. There is a pixie element in the plainest life, and it was Hassan of Bagdad, forty, fat and greasy, who set out to journey.

> "Always a little further; it may be
> Beyond that last blue mountain barred with snow,
> Across that angry or that glimmering sea.

On Noises in the Night

To approach the subject unequivocally: How many archae-opteryxes did it take to form one bird? — for in reality this is a problem in evolution. The primitive simplicity of Eden forbade the double life. People in these aeons respected the proprieties, and retired from publicity with the sun. Night was equivalent to silence (except for an insignificant howl or so, ignored by the innocent sleepers); till a man of greater genius than his fellows (an amorous lover, perhaps: or a lean and hungry Cassius) discovered the immeasurable superiority of the night for secrecy and wile; a discovery whose development (the nemesis of all discoveries) has proved its own undoing. From that time on the long-suffering world has witnessed a crescendo of Night Noises — the grating of steel, the thud of the baton, the rattle of chains, the click of the pistol, the police-man's whistle, the shriek of the locomotive, the screech of the motor-siren, the brr-r-r of the aeroplane — all the braggadocio and pomposity of super civilisation.

These, however, are false Florimels, artificial noises, parvenus, not to be taken account of in the ancient aristocracy of Nature. Your true and aboriginal noise, in comparison with these brazen upstarts, is elusive, only to be apprehended by the nice discrimination of an attentive ear. George MacDonald's position granted — "Of noise alone is born the inward sense of silence" — the converse is equally true. Night by poetic justice belongs to the connoisseur in noises. Then only can he discern each in its elemental nature, detecting its peculiar essence — tasting sounds, as it were, with the relish of a gourmet and the avidity of Sancho Panza in the wilderness. Not only the silence of night, but its darkness, favours him. That busybody, the curious and peeping eye, is perforce idle; and the acknowledged acuteness of hearing in the blind is only a specialised instance of a universal truth.

The wind is responsible for much in the economy of night-hearkening: and noises unperceived by day, at night take on gigantic proportions. It is not the creaking of a door, or the rattling of a window, or the ominous tapping of branches, or the whistle of the gale at street-corners, or its moaning insistence in the chimney — it is none of these things that hurls us back through centuries and strips us naked to our elemental superstitious selves. It is the accident that they happen in the night. Ghost stories may conceivably be the monstrous progeny of this union of Night and Wind. It was wrong to assume that the caveman slept soundly through the dark. They listened to noises, if they did not make them; we are usually so busy making them that we forget to listen. When we do listen, we too are caveman, re-living part of our telescoped experience. Night, that sets the puny world in its true perspective with regard to the illimitable universe, shatters the illusion of modernity and reveals us to ourselves in our primeval agelessness.

Schools and Schoolmistresses

All schools are not so big as the High School. There are a good many in Scotland that consist of a single room. They lie in glens and islands, remote outskirts of the country such as that described the other week by a little girl, in an essay on her home, as "the farrest back place in the world." Geographically, she meant on the edges of the earth — an islet off the western shore of Lewis. The mother tongue for the bairns there is Gaelic. They come to school innocent of English. The teacher, a Gaelic speaker herself, must harden her heart and pretend not to understand the answers to her English questions that come so readily in the Island speech. When the stories she tells in English are retold by the children, the results are strange. "Adam and Ebe libe in a shoe," they tell her.

I receive letters from many such schools; some I have visited, to numerous others I am invited. One old student writes, "I am settling in now to my schoolhouse. By next summer I'll have furniture enough for a visitor. It's thirty miles from the port, but I've a mo-bike and side-car. I'll meet you at the boat." Another says, "Just you wait till I get some sticks into that schoolhouse of mine and pull up a few of the weeds, and we'll see what the air of Glen — will do for you." It was this young teacher who, when I went to see her, looked critically at my feet. I was

133

wearing strong brown brogues and passed the scrutiny. Look at mine, she said, "Mens. I always buy men's shoes now. Nothing else is any use. The school is off the road, you see. Just a cart track along the side of the field. I've wet feet for six months at a stretch."

To reach another I tramp five miles up the glen, knapsack on back. I sleep on an improvised bed in the parlour — the girl would gladly give me her own bed but she has to share it with another lodger, there is nowhere else to stay. In the morning I go to school with her, tell some stories to her bairns, and tramp twelve miles across the hills to another railway line. For nine out of the twelve miles there is not a single house.

Some of these girls live alone in their schoolhouses, doing for themselves. In one larger school I know, three teachers live together and do their own work. The home of one of these is eight miles away, and at the weekends she goes home to her widowed mother. At places she has to kilt her coats and wade — or else go round an extra three miles. Last year a post fell vacant close to her home. She applied, and failed because she had no cookery qualification. "After doing all our own cooking for seven years!" she wrote to me. "Next time I send in an application I'm going to include a specimen of my Scotch broth." But Scotch broth in the hand is not worth a bushel of certificates.

Consider the life of these girls. Many of them come from country homes. They spend some years at a Junior Student centre and two (if they are non-graduates) as students in a busy city. Then they drift into their corner: and often stay there. There may or may not be a few persons in the vicinity with interests beyond the local news. There will possibly be some form of library, say under the Carnegie Trust. There may be the "Rural". There will be the same faces and same phrases and same limited succession of duties year after year. It is for girls like these that summer vacation courses are so admirable. They are not only kept in touch with the newest developments and ideas in their profession, but for three weeks or a month they are quickened and stimulated by the pressure of eager life. They are part of a crowd; and a crowd that is seeking the same ends as themselves. They experience again that undercurrent of intellectual excitement that makes of student life a perpetual adventure.

How appalling the isolation is to which a young teacher may be subjected was brought home to me forcibly when I was visiting an old student in a small town on the west coast. Six miles inland from the head of the loch, a wet valley has been dammed across to provide water power for electricity. The water is carried down through a row of 4-ft pipes. We walked one day to the dam, which runs six more miles into the hills. The first two miles were by road, the rest of the way there was not even a path. We could walk on the pipes or on the rough, wet and very steep hillsides. Sometimes we came to foaming burns which could be crossed only on top of the pipes. At the sluice there was one habitation; and the man in charge had three children. How were these bairns educated? They could not possibly walk to school. For a while the Education Authority appointed a young teacher to stay in the house and teach them. But what girl would stay there? Wet hills, streaming waterfalls, gigantic peaks, six miles of water where, when the level was lowered, there could be seen the chimney of a shepherd's house that had once stood in the valley: spiritual isolation. I walked twice down the pipe-track and on both occasions my shoes were sopping. That was in September. What of midwinter? At last the Authority paid the father (a man of sufficient education) to give regular instruction to his own youngsters.

Teaching practice in city schools is not a full preparation for such a life. There are differences between a class of fifty children of the same age and a whole school numbering twenty. Three years ago, for the first time in Scotland, the Aberdeen Training Centre instituted a model Rural school. In two rooms of the building two teachers, experienced in rural work, teach three classes simultaneously. The conditions of course cannot be identical, for these are city children artificially segregated from a mass of others of the same age and attainments with whom they will again consort out of class hours; but the student can at least learn how to manipulate several classes at once and arrange a scheme of work to include them all. Yet there a hundred things besides that no Training College can teach; things that depend on the relation between a single teacher and the tiny community of which she forms part. And that relation in its turn depends on the individual.

Here is a lady. You would open your eyes to see her school. The room is fresh and dainty; there are flowers and pictures. The children arrive, a rough set, from cottar homes. Each child immediately changes into slippers; when the inspector visits, each has a buttonhole. This teacher has just been transferred. The girl who is to occupy her post says to me, "I'll never live up to yon. I'll not even be able to throw a lump of coal on the fire with my fingers."

And I must tell of the girl whose landlady serves rabbit for dinner every day of the week for most months of the year: sometimes tufts of fur are floating in the soup. But there is no other house that will take a lodger and the rabbits are at the back door ... Nor have I told of the lassie who helps in the local "shoppie" on Saturday nights. "It's fine fun" she says, "you meet the company". Nor of the landlady who runs a baby-farm, and, called away on urgent business one Saturday, left the seven bairns in charge of the "teacherie". Nor of the ... But there are too many such stories, and some of the strangest I must not tell.

The Old Wives

They last longer than the men. Or last better. In this part of the country at any rate. One sees old men grow decrepit, all fail, take to their beds and keep there, or crawl the earth, tottering monuments, death's heads between two sticks. But the old women stand erect. They rise before the light, make fires, milk cows. They drag firewood from the hill, stew tea and drink it — black as peat, strong as their own sinewy selves. They speak tersely, not with the gossiping ineptitude of ancient men, they delve, they sweat, they hurl the barrow, they scorn the saving of labour and think leisure a Deil's trap for the empty-headed. They hold by tradition with a serene certainty of its endurance. When I consider the magnificent procession of old women I have known, of my own knowledge, in my own lifetime, within the limits of a couple of Scottish counties, I recognise how hardy change can beat them. If the Devil or Jehovah himself, wants to alter Scotland by means of a revolution, he will have his own ado. The old women will bide as they are. Anyone who likes may have the last word, they will have the last act, and it will be to turn the teapot round and stew the other half of the tea.

There is Miss Abercrombie Gaunt, hard as a harrow. In my

childhood I thought someone must lay her into bed, all of a piece. I see her always standing up. Perhaps she sits down, but I can't understand how. Her skirts droop at the back, invariably, just as Betsy's bunch out always from her ample waist, six inches above her sturdy ankles. By their shapes shall you know them. Miss Abercrombie's clothes-pole figure has stalked for fifty years, wet and dry, the five miles from her home to town and the five miles back: on Fridays to market, on Thursdays to shop, on Saturdays to walk the meaner streets and wrestle in speech with the drunken, on Sundays to walk the parks and wrestle with the idle, on Mondays to visit one hospital, on Tuesdays, another on Wednesdays — bless me if I remember what she did on Wednesdays but are there not prisons, parks, beaches, promenades and pubs? Somewhere she went, that is certain. I smile when I read of all the Movements it has required to oust women from the domestic duties. Miss Abercrombie required only herself.

Then Betsy. Betsy is hoarse, and black. Her nails are encrusted with earth. She dargs like a man. I have seen Betsy with split and bleeding fingers build up a fallen dyke. I have seen her clamber (at sixty-nine) on her cottage roof and renew the thatch. Indoors the work is done by her brother-in-law, a meek man. "Ach, a kindly craitur" Betsy says. "Ill-less, guidless." Out of work, out of home, Betsy in her goodness allows him to keep her house. You enter, and in the shining kitchen he creeps away, silent as pussy, apologetic. Yet you remember that before he came, the kitchen never shone, the hearth was grey, rubbish piled itself in corners. The apology, you feel, should not be wholly his. But win him to talk and there is no reward. His talk is flat and poor, while Betsy's harsh voice exalts you like a dram.

I have not discovered what Betsy's dead sister was like ...

And Mrs. Martin. At seventy-three she discusses with her grandson the points of his latest motor-byke but do not think that she is a modern. She knows the workings of the fleet of motor lorries that carries her milk and butter to-day just as she knew about harness and horseshoes in her early married life and for the same reason — that lorry driver and horseman are alike under her rule, and the universe she rules must hold no mysteries for her. Mrs. Martin is a formidable lady. She has done so much good in the district that I am afraid to think about it. Her advice is so excellent that I shouldn't dare to ask for any. Her services to the community are numberless and she does them all so splendidly — her figure is noble, her skirts fall like the Queen's.

But my deepest affection is given to the old woman whom the children call Lintie. I don't know why. She cannot sing and her name is plain Miss Mair. But *Lintie* expresses the tenderness, the freshness and delight that dwell in her heart. Her body is twisted, she is seldom out of pain but never out of reach. She is accessible to all who want her, and the children want her often. Her needle is always theirs. They believe implicitly that there is nothing she cannot mend. Mend, make, remake, fashion to unexpected use. The dolls and toys for miles around visit Lintie — she can heal them all. And each new problem that comes to her she treats with the solemnity it deserves. Is it not all a part of creation, and infinitely new?

Things I Shall Never Know

To-day I waited for my bus beside a modiste's window. A voice said at my ear: "Excuse me, but would you tell me if that coat has ermine on the sleeves as well as the collar." I turned and saw a round red face, one eye covered with a patch, the other inflamed and peering — a shabby black coat, a dowdy hat. Inside the window lay the coat. It was an elegant coat. I described it carefully. She peered again, asked another question. Then she thanked me, saying, "you must do something to smarten yourself up a bit, when you haven't much money," and went her way.

Bless her. May the coat prosper.

But I shall never see it.

* * *

I leaned on a gate in a gap of the hedge. Sheep were in the field behind me, a Dorsetshire lane behind. Suddenly in the field a voice began to speak. I had come to those parts only the day before and the Dorset intonation beat me. I listened, trying idly to recognise even one word. And just then the man came

140

out towards the gap and saw me. He was a big handsome man, straight and weather-beaten; and at the sight of me he blushed through his tan. "I didn't know a lady was there," he said. "I was speaking to the sheep." When he wasn't speaking to the sheep his English was plain enough and we have a *newse*. Very pleasant fellow.

But I have never known what he was apologising for.

★   ★   ★

July. The London train, which I had joined somewhere in the Midlands, was very late. I was turned out at a junction, my connection lost. Another woman, in the same plight as I, sat motionless on a station seat. I went for a walk, returned, she still sat motionless. A big untidy paper parcel lay on her knee, another at her feet. I gave her chocolate and she gave me her life history: how her husband beat her (she looked about twenty) and deserted her, and how she made her living in an eating-house near the London Docks and her employer had suddenly said that morning that she might have a holiday; and how she had just caught the train and here she was, dead beat. And she discussed employers with me, and hours, and husbands, and she asked, "Are you in service too?" and I felt glad to be accepted as of her own kind.

Then our train came in and we boarded it. She talked on — suddenly I saw the name of a station. "Thornet Junction — isn't that where you said you had to get out?" "Is it? Do I get out here?" she asked in a helpless fashion. "Yes, you said Thornet, didn't you?" I bundled her out, parcels and all, just as the train was moving, and she looked back at me with a pale grateful smile — five minutes later the train stopped again. "Thornet."

My heart turned over. Thornet? Thornet Junction? She was to catch a bus at Thornet. Had I turned her out at the wrong place?

I shall never know; but there are still times when I wake in the night, remembering her white weary face, and wonder.

★ ★ ★

A winter morning, 5.30 or thereby, dark, dismal. Perth Railway Station. Change for Aberdeen. The passengers are pouring along the platform, fast, escaping from the chill dreariness of travel. But at one point there is a knot. Three porters, a ticket collector, a taxi-driver, are gathered round a French-woman in deep mourning and tears. She talks, they talk. French, Scots. Impasse. I talk — she turns, she is fervent. Ah, someone who can understand her plight! She knows no English, has never before left France. Her husband was to have met her — he is not here. She asks me, what is there to do? But has she not Monsieur's address? Address? Ah yes, she has an address — but she cannot use it. Two ticket collectors, four porters, and the taxi-driver thrust a piece of paper upon me. "What would you make o' that, Miss?" The handwriting is very French. I can make no good Scots of it at all. As I am puzzling it out, comes a commotion. I look up, the porters, ticket collectors, taxi-driver, have parted, and down the platform is running a man. He is a middle-aged Frenchman, dapper, black-bearded, and he runs as I have never seen any man run in the flesh but only on the screen — left, right, left, right, a beautiful symmetry of mechanism. Madame holds out her arms, he falls into them, peck, peck, this cheek, that cheek, this cheek, that cheek. Torrents of French. Then as they move away, Madame's voice, gay and clear, "Et ce sacré Bart-tolomew Road — où donc ça?"

Works in the order printed here

'Descent from the Cross', *Scots Magazine,* 1943

'Colours of Deeside', *The Deeside Field,* 1938

'Wild Geese in Glen Callater', *The Deeside Field,* 1959

'The Lupin Island', *The Deeside Field,* 1965

'James McGregor and the Downies of Braemar', *The Deeside Field,*
    1962

'Achiltibuie', 4th October 1950

'Next Morning', 5th October 1950

'On a Still Morning', 6th October 1950

'Rhu Coigach', October 1950

'Falketind', July 1937

'The Trees', May 1918

'Underground', 1918

'The Dryad', 1918

'Arthur's Seat', July 1919

'The Burning Glass', May 1921

'Union', c. 1931

'Street Urchins', August 1919

'The Poetry of Hugh MacDiarmid', *Aberdeen University Review*, November 1938

'Marion Angus', *Scots Magazine*, 1947

'Charles Murray', *Hamewith: the Complete Poems of Charles Murray*, 1979

'Smuts', *Saturday Westminster Gazette*, 1916

'Pixies and Or'nary Peoples', *Aberdeen High School Magazine*, c. 1919

'On Noises in the Night', *Saturday Westminster Gazette*, 1915

'Schools and Schoolmistresses', MS 2744, National Library of Scotland, Edinburgh.

'The Old Wives', MS 2744, National Library of Scotland, Edinburgh

'Things I Shall Never Know', *Gala Rag*, 1934

'Achiltibuie' appeared first in Roderick Watson's foreword to *A Pass in the Grampians* in 1996. It was also reproduced along with 'Next Morning', 'On a Still Morning' and 'Rhu Coigach' in Charlotte Peacock: *Into the Mountain: A Life of Nan Shepherd* in 2017.

'The Trees', 'Underground' and 'Union', appeared first in Charlotte Peacock: *Into the Mountain: A Life of Nan Shepherd* in 2017.

'Falketind', 'The Dryad', 'Arthur's Seat' and 'The Burning Glass' are published here for the first time.

'Charles Murray: An Appreciation' appeared first in *Charles Murray: The Last Poems* in 1969.

Notes

Warm thanks are due to:

Erlend Clouston and the Nan Shepherd Estate for their support and permission to reproduce the works in this volume; the Trustees of the National Library of Scotland; the University of Aberdeen's Special Collections; Dairmid Gunn for permission to quote from unpublished letters. Sources for material quoted in the Introduction are given below.

Endnotes

1   Robert Dunnett, 'Nan Shepherd: One of the Scottish "Moderns"', *The Scotsman,* July 1933.

2   Coley Taylor, *Duttons Weekly News,* 1928, MS 27443/5, National Library of Scotland, Edinburgh.

3   Elizabeth Kyle, 'Modern Women Authors', *Scots Observer,* June 1931.

4   Rachel Annand Taylor to Nan Shepherd, 30 Aug 1959, MS 3036, Special Collections, University of Aberdeen.

5   Sheila Hamilton, 'Writer of genius gave up', *Evening Express* (Aberdeen) 15 Dec 1976.

6   Nan Shepherd, 'Wild Geese in Glen Callater', p. 75

7   Agnes Mure Mackenzie to Nan Shepherd, 19 May 1926, MS 2750, Special Collections, University of Aberdeen.

8   Nan Shepherd, 'James McGregor and the Downies of Braemar', p. 68

9   Nan Shepherd, 'Marion Angus', p. 120

10   Nan Shepherd, 'Charles Murray', p. 130

11   Nan Shepherd, 'The Old Wives', p. 149

12   Nan Shepherd, 'James McGregor and the Downies of Braemar', p. 70

13   Nan Shepherd, 'The Colours of Deeside', p. 54

14   Nan Shepherd, 'Wild Geese in Glen Callater', p. 75

15   Nan Shepherd, 'Descent from the Cross', p. 21.

16   Neil Gunn to Nan Shepherd, 26 Jul 1943, MS 15520, National
     Library of Scotland, Edinburgh.

17   Nan Shepherd to Neil Gunn, 14 Mar 1930, Deposit 209, Box 19,
     Folder 7, National Library of Scotland, Edinburgh.

18   Nan Shepherd to Neil Gunn, 2 Apr 1931, Deposit 209, Box 19,
     Folder 7, National Library of Scotland, Edinburgh.

19   ibid.

20   Nan Shepherd to Neil Gunn, 15 Sep 1931, Deposit 209, Box 19,
     Folder 7, National Library of Scotland, Edinburgh.

21   Sheila Hamilton, 'Writer of genius gave up', *Evening Express*
     (Aberdeen) 15 Dec 1976.

22   The sonnet, 'Without My Right', published in *In the Cairngorms,* was
     originally titled 'Illicit Love' see Nan Shepherd's manuscript, MS
     27442, National Library of Scotland, Edinburgh.

23   Nan Shepherd, 'The Burning Glass', p. 90.

24   Nan Shepherd, *The Living Mountain,* (Edinburgh: Canongate, 2011) p. 108.

25   Nan Shepherd to Neil Gunn, 5 Jun 1937, Deposit 209, Box 19,
     Folder 7, National Library of Scotland, Edinburgh.

26   Nan Shepherd, 'Achiltibuie', p. TBA.

27   Nan Shepherd, 'Wild Geese of Glen Callater', p. 74

28   Nan Shepherd, 'On Noises in the Night', p. 143

29   'Miss Anna Shepherd: Women Citizens', MS 27443, National Library
     of Scotland, Edinburgh.

30   Nan Shepherd, *The Quarry Wood,* (Edinburgh: Canongate, 1996) p. 208.

31   Elizabeth Kyle, 'Modern Women Authors', *Scots Observer,* June 1931.

32   Nan Shepherd to Neil Gunn, 14 Mar 1930, Deposit 209, Box 19,
     Folder 7, National Library of Scotland, Edinburgh.

33   Nan Shepherd, *The Living Mountain* (Edinburgh: Canongate, 2011) p. 105.